SRH

Roscommon County Library

3 0001 00203 673 5

ATE

D0548314

No Range Is Free

No Range Is Free

E. E. Halleran

Roscommon County Library Service

WITHDRAWN
FROM STOCK

Sagebrush
Large Print Westerns

Copyright © 1944 by Eugene Edward Halleran
Copyright © renewed 1972 by Eugene Edward Halleran

First published in the United States by Macrae Smith

First published in Great Britain by ISIS Publishing Ltd

Published in Large Print 2004 by ISIS Publishing Ltd,
7 Centremead, Osney Mead, Oxford OX2 0ES,
United Kingdom
by arrangement with
Golden West Literary Agency

All rights reserved

The moral right of the author has been asserted

British Library Cataloguing in Publication Data
Halleran, E. E.
    No range is free. – Large print ed. –
    (Sagebrush western series)
    1. Western stories
    2. Large type books
    I. Title
    813.5'4 [F]

ISBN 0–7531–7124–4 (hb)

Printed and bound by Antony Rowe, Chippenham

CHAPTER
ONE

The full flavor of spring was in the gathering dusk as Tom Shelby eased his pony down the cutbank into Moccasin Valley. Earthy smells, newly released from winter bondage, rose on the warm breeze and Shelby filled his lungs gratefully. Spring always brought a tinge of excitement to him — and this was a very special Spring. This one would mark the end of Tom Shelby, trapper, and a beginning for Tom Shelby, ranchman. The two pack horses behind him carried the fruits of his winter's toil, a stake which would bring his savings to the dignity of Capital.

The horses moved forward eagerly as they reached the flat, more concerned with the smell of water than with the damp scents of earth and pine which had interested the man. A bullfrog boomed in the creek shallows, his basso quickly punctuated by a splash as the horses thrust dusty muzzles into the brawling stream. It was good to be down from the mountains and the lanky rider wasn't the only one who was enjoying it.

Shelby swung stiffly from the saddle and drank, wiping the icy drops from bearded lips with an impatient backhand. It was time to camp for the night

1

and he found himself resenting the necessity. Now that he was so close to his destination it was irritating to delay. The winter was over. He had his stake and there was free range to be had for the taking. It was time for action.

He slapped a lean hand gently against the shoulder of his saddle horse. "Easy there, Useless," he warned, his voice gruffly soothing. "You'll founder yourself on so much water. Back outa there before you get a belly-ache!"

The big roan backed obediently, snorting only a mild protest as he hauled the pack horses back from the water.

"Good hoss," Shelby approved when the animals were lined up again. "Now let's see what we'd better do." He continued to pat the roan's neck in a gesture of absent-minded caress. It went against the grain to call a halt but already the pines were looming black against a darkening sky. A prudent man would make camp right away.

"How about it, Useless?" he asked, lips close to the ear of the big horse. "Shall we call it a day or shall we push on down the valley? Old Bear Nose's village ought to be somewhere close."

Useless nickered gently, wet muzzle upthrust into the warm wind. Shelby chuckled, partly at the roan's apparent understanding and partly at his own words. Whenever he was in doubt about anything he always confided in Useless. It helped his thought processes — and Useless didn't seem to mind.

"I reckon you're right, boy," he said, as though the roan's reply had been fully intelligible. "We better stick to the trail. This weather is sure to be a storm breeder. Too warm for this time o' year and I've got a notion some of that darkness behind the ridge ain't just plain night. Maybe we'd better shove on down the gulch to where we can find some shelter if things start to bust loose overhead."

He laughed aloud. "There! I reckon we argued ourselves into that!" Still laughing at himself he threw a long leg over the saddle and clucked to Useless. All of that argument had been more or less true but he recognized the real reason behind his own rationalization. He simply wanted to keep moving.

There was a trail of a sort and Useless set off at a good pace, seeming to understand that there would be no rest until Shelby could find no further excuse for pushing ahead. They had gone something under a half mile when a puff of cooler air suddenly met them — bringing the disquieting sound of rifle fire. Shelby pulled up abruptly, realizing that the shots must have drifted up the valley from the village he was expecting to visit. Not a fight, judging from the brevity of the shooting, but enough excitement to make a white man proceed with plenty of caution.

The roan was listening with his lanky master. Shelby rubbed the animal's neck reassuringly and murmured, "Reckon we'd better stop here, hoss, while I go have a look-see. It don't sound like a very healthy time to go blunderin' into a Cheyenne village. I've got three good ponies, a nice pile of furs and a handsome scalp that

I'm real choice of. No sense in danglin' 'em before the eyes of a bunch of locoed heathens."

He recalled the rumors of trouble he had heard last autumn, just before moving out to his trap lines. Maybe General Sherman's treaty had been scrapped — as had happened to so many other papers of its kind. The young bucks had a nasty habit of ignoring tribal promises — just as the land-hungry settlers wouldn't abide by the guarantees of the Indian Office. Much could have happened during the winter, and a little caution never hurt anyone.

He grimaced slightly at the thought. In the past, Tom Shelby had never been particularly noted for his caution. Maybe the prospect of settling down and becoming a rancher was putting some sense into his head.

He led the three horses into a pine thicket where the trees concealed the sheer rise of the canyon wall. "You rascals wait here," he said as he picketed them securely. "It smells rainy so maybe you'll get a mite damp before I come back, but it'll be better than losing a fine, good-lookin' master like me. You wouldn't like the job of haulin' Cheyenne lodges around the prairie anyway."

Checking his position carefully he moved back into the open and headed down the valley on foot. It was a relief to stretch those long legs again after a hard day's ride but there was little time for him to enjoy the exercise. As if the threat of trouble were not enough, a distant flare of lightning slashed the sky behind the ridge. It illuminated a vast bank of rolling clouds which seemed to be driving up the valley with plenty of wind

4

behind them. Mother Nature was about to take her revenge for this precocious exhibition of Spring.

For a moment Shelby was tempted to go back for the horses but a deeper sense of danger warned him against it. His route lay through Moccasin Valley and he had to know more about conditions before he presumed on the friendliness of the Cheyennes ahead. The weather was threatening but the risk of storm was a trifle as compared to what might happen if the tribes were up.

The cool breeze stopped almost as suddenly as it had begun, a dead calm suffocating the valley as Shelby moved along. The ominous silence was broken at intervals by the distant rumbling of thunder but more disquieting was the sound of drumming and shouting which the trapper could now hear so plainly. The Cheyennes were certainly excited about something — and it wasn't the approaching storm.

He plunged on grimly, black night having settled full upon the valley by the time he came within sight of the thirty-odd skin tepees which nestled beneath a craggy bluff. Arranged in the traditional circle they indicated a camp of perhaps seventy warriors — but fully a hundred were even now cavorting about a huge central fire. The fantastic ceremonies of the war dance were in progress, the drumming, shouting and occasional shots indicating only too well that the frenzy was approaching some sort of climax.

Shelby watched for some moments from a respectful distance, aware that the Cheyennes were not alone in their village. A band of Arapahos were prominent in the prancing circle while two greasy Kiowas stood at one side beating time. Even a half dozen Oglala Sioux shook their feathered crows in the wild abandon of the dance.

That looked bad. Oglalas didn't come this far south unless something big was afoot, nor did they fraternize with the Cheyennes unless there was a common enemy of great importance. This war dance indicated something big. Maybe the long-feared Indian war was at hand with all the tribes arrayed against the white man.

Shelby grunted under his breath, less concerned over his immediate safety than with the future trouble he could foresee. If the tribes were up his careful plans would have to be scrapped. Even if he could manage to get his pelts through to Fort Butler it would be unsafe to venture back into the hills this year. Ranch building in Moccasin Valley would not be healthy with an Indian war getting started.

The thought made him the more curious about the scene in front of him. Bear Nose was a blanket Indian but a remarkably peaceful one. He had always been friendly with the white people — and bitterly hostile to the Sioux. What had happened that his village should now be the scene of such riotous activity?

It didn't take Tom long to discover that Bear Nose was not in the circle of warriors. A quarter of the way around the ring of lodges could be seen a tepee bearing the crest of the venerable chief but Bear Nose himself was not in sight. A squatty warrior named Bull Horn seemed to be directing the show and Shelby wondered if Bear Nose had been the victim of some upheaval in tribal politics.

He caught a flicker of movement at the door of Bear Nose's lodge and in the glare of the firelight he recognized the features of the old man's second squaw. Even at the distance he could see that she was troubled. She seemed to be talking with someone behind her and Shelby suddenly thought he could read the picture. Bear Nose had lost control of his warriors and was saving his face by staying out of sight, leaving the squaw to report developments to him.

Shelby hesitated only briefly, then he began to make his way around the circle toward Bear Nose's tepee, well aware that discovery would mean sure — but not sudden — death. Maybe it would be the part of wisdom to get away quickly but he decided to gamble. He wanted to know more about this mess and there was a fair chance that he could learn something from Bear Nose. There had been a real bond of affection between him and the chief, a bond which should now be particularly strong if Bear Nose had become angry with his warriors. Getting into the old man's lodge would be risky in the extreme but Shelby determined to make the effort.

Taking full advantage of every shadow he began to circle the village, pleased to note that the Indians and their dogs were all occupied with the excitement of the dance. That was fine. Now he wouldn't have to worry about stray village curs betraying him.

He had moved some fifty feet away from the valley trail when the noise of hoofbeats sounded behind him.

He flattened himself in a thick clump of pines, fearful that he might be silhouetted against the firelight. A fresh puff of wind swept up the valley to meet the new arrivals and Tom realized with a flash of relief that it was sprinkling rain. This new party would be facing the shower as they rode, a pretty good assurance that they would not have been too observant of any odd shadows around the village.

The savages at the fire halted their dancing and waited. For an instant Tom was fearful that they might rush to meet the newcomers, thus exposing him to discovery, but the riders came on too swiftly. To the accompaniment of rolling thunder a small band of mounted warriors dashed into camp from the same direction Tom had previously come. A dozen Cheyennes and a trio of Kiowas galloped their ponies into the circle of firelight, three horses in their midst bearing limp burdens. Two of these were dead Cheyennes but the third was a bound prisoner. A white woman!

Shelby swore gently. His problem had become complicated. He knew he could never leave this valley without making some attempt to rescue that prisoner.

CHAPTER
TWO

The woman's face was hidden beneath the buffalo hood but Tom felt certain of her identity. She must be the wife of that Swede immigrant who had come into the hills last summer. Shelby remembered hearing talk of the strange settler, a silent man who had been the butt of endless rough jokes at Sheridan. Apparently the man had brought his wife along just in time to meet trouble.

Tom watched grimly while the woman was dragged from her horse and thrown bodily into a tepee which stood beneath the overhanging cliff. There was no need to visit Bear Nose now. This move answered all the questions. The tribes were on the warpath, attacking settlers who had been friendly.

He flattened himself against the ground as a brighter blaze of lightning illuminated the valley. The storm was coming over fast but its approach was welcomed by the trapper. It might give him the opportunity to do the impossible.

He worked back across the trail, keeping an eye on the captive's tepee as he circled the village. As yet there had been no sign of any Indians around the lodge. With any luck he might find her alone. Under cover of the storm he might be able to . . . well, a man could only try!

Rain beat down in increasing volume, breaking up the celebration in the village, but Tom was pleased to note that no warriors took refuge in the tepee where the woman had been placed. He bent his head to the storm, wondering whether he would be doing her any favor to take her out into the hills on a night like this. After all, the Cheyennes were notably decent toward women prisoners.

It was only a thought. Then he was crawling forward, shivering a little as the storm brought a blast of cold air. Guided by the rapid flares of lightning he had moved well around the ring of lodges when suddenly the earth shuddered under the impact of a tremendous bolt of fire. Half blinded and partly stunned, he could still see the streak of white flame which seemed to skid down a tall pine and jump to the peak of the tepee which housed the white woman.

A wail of terror arose on all sides as the concussion died away. Little fires broke out in several places, only to be quickly smothered by the deluge. Shelby stared dazedly, trying to rally his senses. Then another flash showed him the havoc wrought by that terrifying bolt. The prisoner's tepee had simply ceased to exist, only a steaming heap of rubble marking the spot where it had been. Tom thought he could distinguish a body in the ruins but it was impossible to be certain. Already the Indians were edging out of their lodges to stare fearfully at the scene of destruction. With something of grim

10

relief in his grunt of horror, Shelby turned and ran headlong before the storm.

That last shattering impact had relieved him of his responsibility but it had also loosened the floodgates of the skies. Pelting rain, whirled between canyon walls, seemed to drive at him from all sides on the wings of the gale. He ran with his head down, still holding his gun in his hand and making no attempt at concealment. His first sprint turned into a stumbling trot as the rain combined with the darkness to blind him but his spirits rose quickly. He had been wet many times before. That was a small matter compared to the relative safety which the storm had brought. No war parties would be on the trail tonight.

He hurried along over the rocks and through the bushes, trying to pick out the opening which he knew marked a trail over the ridge. He had never used it but he knew that it was there and tonight he would have to find it in the dark. It was a roundabout road to Fort Butler, the road he would have to use now that Buffalo Pass and the Moccasin were closed to him.

The lightning was coming less frequently now but after a while he spotted the ford and the beaten path up the opposite bank of the creek. That would be the trail to White Water Valley, the trail which had just been covered by the unfortunate prisoner and her savage captors. Somewhere at the end of it would be a dead man and the ruins of a frontier home but it should now be clear of warriors. They had already done their dirty work in that quarter.

A scant half mile beyond he managed to locate the thicket where he had left the horses. The pack animals had tried to stampede at the approach of the storm and were thoroughly snarled in their lead ropes. Now they stood helplessly, tail to the wind, waiting. Useless whinnied gently at Tom's approach and the trapper set to work without delay, trying to calm and soothe the animals with his voice as he untangled the mess in the darkness.

It was a tedious job but eventually the pack animals were ready for the trail once more. Shelby swung into the wet saddle and urged Useless toward the trail. "Time to move on, partner," he said softly. "I hate to do this to you fellers but the orders call for a forced march. Let's get a wiggle on!"

The rain had settled into a steady downpour but Tom didn't mind that. He knew where he was going now. He located the ford without delay and Useless struck out obediently into the shallow but rising creek. They found the trail on the other side and Shelby let the reins go slack as the horse began to climb. "Your trail now, hoss," he muttered. "Don't get us lost!"

The big roan seemed to understand. At any rate he started off as though determined to do what was expected of him. Most of the time Shelby could see nothing but the dark bulk of the pine-clad heights above him, depending entirely on the instinct of the big horse to find the trail. Then the storm doubled back and the man was able to watch progress by the light of brilliant jets of fire which spouted from the lowering clouds.

12

Several times he stopped to rest the weary animals but by the time the storm had passed they were well into the notch, apparently near the crest of the ridge. An hour later a few reappearing stars disclosed the fact that they were working their way down into a gulch which must lead into White Water Valley. Tom shivered miserably in the saddle but urged the horses onward. Every mile he could cover before daylight was a valuable step toward safety.

In places the trail ran across soggy carpets of pine needles while in other places it was simply a thread of treacherous slime along a craggy ledge where a single slip would mean disaster. The horses slogged along wearily, showing signs of breaking as they neared the limits of their endurance.

Shelby let them rest more frequently now but never for very long. It was a grim business and there was no time for delay.

A faint suspicion of gray had crept into the dripping east when the trail finally leveled off into a narrow valley. With the dawn the rain came back for one last flurry, then the last wisps of clouds dropped behind the ridge, bringing scant comfort to the man who had been thoroughly soaked for so many hours. He urged the animals out across the widening flat only to pull up in dismay as he caught the tang of wood smoke.

It would be fatal to run across more raiders now, a brutal irony after the trouble he had taken to get here. He started to wheel his horse but checked himself as the realization came home to him that there could be but one fire here. Nothing but the smouldering ruins of the immigrant's cabin could have survived such a downpour as the night had produced.

He dismounted, however, leading the horses forward until he came within sight of the blackened embers which had so recently been the home of the man who called the Cheyennes friends. No human figure was in sight but Shelby continued his cautious progress, his gun held ready.

Suddenly Useless halted abruptly, ears thrust forward in evident alarm.

"What's wrong, boy?" Shelby murmured, tired eyes searching the adjacent clearing and the woodland beyond. "Smell a wolf, do you?"

No real thought of a wolf entered his mind but it was like him to discount danger, even to a horse. He took another pace forward, pulling Useless along. Then he saw it, a charred body lying in the ashes.

"Steady, boy," he soothed. "Nothin' there to hurt us. Just a poor devil with more sand than sense." The man had met much the same fate as had his unfortunate wife on the other side of the ridge.

Shelby turned the roan's head with a quick gesture as he vaulted into the saddle. "Let's slope, Useless. You're tired, I know, but this is no place for a man with a quick stomach and a hankerin' for his hair."

Useless seemed willing. He even tried a weary trot as they headed down the valley but the drag of the pack animals quickly brought him to a walk. They moved toward a break in the woods where a path seemed to follow the roiled waters of a sizeable stream. That would be the trail down White Water Creek, a road to safety if further war parties could be avoided.

For all his weariness he could appreciate the beauty of the valley. The squarehead had certainly picked a fine site for a ranch, just as good a spot as Tom had already selected over in the Moccasin. The choice hadn't done him much good, however, and Tom wondered if his own plans were to suffer such a rude reverse.

The momentary abstraction almost made him miss the footprints at the trail's edge. There were just a few of them showing in a patch of bare mud but they told their story. Shelby's face was suddenly haggard as he looked up from studying them. This time it was no false alarm. He had ridden all night just to stick his head into more trouble. There were moccasin prints, made since that last shower.

"More grief, hoss," he muttered. "Shall we keep on or try to dog it back into the woods?"

He frowned in perplexity as he glanced down again, trying to read the story in the mud. They were not Cheyenne prints. They didn't have the straight side so characteristic of both Cheyenne and Sioux footwear. Too broad a heel for an Arapaho or a Kiowa. Those were the only tribes he had seen represented in the camp of Bear Nose. These prints were more like the Pawnee style — but what would a Pawnee be doing in these hills surrounded by his blood enemies? If the Pawnees had joined in the fight against the whites there must be a real war on!

15

The thought brought his decision. "On we go!" he told Useless grimly. "If it's as bad as that we might as well shove on now and to hell with the risks!"

They moved on into the woodland which now filled the valley but less than a hundred yards had been covered when Shelby's anxious glance caught a flash of movement in the brush ahead. Just around a bend in the trail something gray had flitted across from one side to the other. There was only the briefest glimpse but somehow he knew that the form was human.

He slipped out of the saddle again, his thumb on the hammer of his gun. "Steady, boy," he cautioned, dropping the reins over the roan's head. "Wait here while I take a scout. If there's an ambush up here I'll give 'em plenty of hell before they get me!"

CHAPTER
THREE

He didn't bother to picket the horses, depending on their weariness and Useless's training to keep them close at hand. Plunging straightway into the brush beside the trail he swung in a wide semicircle, slowing only when he had left the path some yards behind. Maybe that shadowy figure had been only a coyote but this was no time to gamble. If a lone Indian was planning an ambush it might be possible to flank him and get rid of him without shooting. Shots had to be avoided if possible.

He crept along through the drenched woodland, his silent movements becoming more ghostlike and deliberate as he swung toward the point where the form had disappeared in the brush. No sound broke the morning stillness except the patter of water dropping from the trees to wet leaves. Shelby cut in toward the trail, every raw nerve alert, but still seeing no trace of an enemy.

"Must have been some kind of an animal," he told himself, almost believing it this time.

Then his glance caught the tiniest flicker of movement in a clump of scrub pines just ahead. He halted, trying to spot the cause. It might be just the

stirring of boughs in the rising breeze or it might be . . .
He advanced warily, taking full advantage of every
cover and moving in absolute silence across the wet
carpet of pine needles.

He was almost among the low, bushy seedlings when
a muffled figure rose before him. The ragged buffalo
hood and small stature proclaimed the unknown to be
a squaw but Shelby was in no mood to take chances.
She was evidently getting up to look out toward the
trail, never suspecting that the rider she had seen was
now directly behind her. Shelby's quick spring gave her
no chance for an outcry, only a startled grunt escaping
from her lips as he bore her to earth, a firm hand tight
across her mouth.

She fought desperately but he worked with efficiency
and speed. Jamming her face into the wet leaves with
his shoulder he pinned both of her arms in a firm grip
and ran his free hand over her clothing in search of
weapons.

Her struggles seemed to weaken after a few moments
and Tom realized that she was smothering, her nose
and mouth buried as it was in the wet leaf mould. By
that time he knew two things: she was unarmed and she
wasn't badly built for a squaw. Probably young, he
decided.

With a quick motion he shoved his hand down into
the muck so as to cover her mouth while he rolled her
over. He didn't know exactly what he was going to do
with her but he couldn't afford to let her make any
outcry. Then as he turned her he saw that she was
white. The face that came up out of the humus was

hardly prepossessing, even after she had wiped the mud away from her mouth, but the pale gold hair left no doubt as to her race.

Tom stared in amazement at the dirty, scratched cheeks and a swollen, battered eye. Releasing her, he stepped back in embarrassment. "Sorry, ma'am," he stammered. "I had you all figured out for a Cheyenne."

She stared at him for a moment or two, trying to get her breath back and biting the torn lips in a stern effort at self-control. Finally her voice came, low but with almost a note of hysteria. "I'm not — and thank God you're not!" She tried to get up but her knees seemed to give way as she made the effort and she sat down heavily in the wet.

Shelby squatted beside her, his voice deliberately casual, trying to calm her even as he urged action. The girl had evidently been through some terrifying experiences and he had no desire to burden himself with an emotionally unstrung refugee. "I don't blame you for sitting down," he said cheerfully — "but we're in a kinda fix. I'm trying to get out of these hills before the red brother decides to keep me for a pet. If you've got anything to offer for the good of the order spill it pronto and we'll hit the trail. Who are you, anyway?"

She stared frowningly at the speech, apparently understanding little except the final question. She took his hand and let him help her up before she made any reply. She was taller than he had at first realized, coming to his chin as she faced him, and he realized that she had a certain air of dignity about her despite the deplorable condition of her face and clothing.

"I'm Karen Neilson," she said finally, her words spoken in the oddly clipped accents of a person who has learned the language from a book. "I lived back there in the valley . . . with my parents. Yesterday the savages came while I was up on the ridge . . . enjoying the sunshine!"

Her voice broke under its load of bitterness and Tom stepped forward a pace, fearing that she might collapse again. She waved him back and went on hurriedly as though determined to take full control of herself.

"We thought the Cheyennes were friendly and I had no fears when I saw them ride into the valley. Then suddenly I saw that Father was running toward the house. The savages began to shoot and Father fell. He was pretty badly wounded, I think, but he managed to regain his feet and stagger into the house. He held them off for a while, killing two, but finally they broke in . . . Then I knew it was all over. After a few minutes they came out, dragging my mother with them. The house was blazing when they rode away."

"When did this happen?" Tom asked.

"Yesterday afternoon. As soon as the Indians left I came down the mountain and tried to put the fire out. It wasn't any use, of course. By that time the whole cabin was ablaze and I didn't even dare go in to get Father's body. I found this old hood hanging on a post where I had left it when the day became warm so I put it on and started down the trail, hoping to reach the fort and get help. I must have fallen on the rocks when it became dark for it was night when I regained my senses to find the rain coming down in torrents. I ached

20

all over and I must have been bewildered for I found myself right back here when daylight came."

Her voice threatened to break again and Tom knew she must be thinking of that blackened corpse back there in the embers. It was remarkable that she could retain any trace of composure after such a night. In spite of his sympathy he felt a quick satisfaction when he realized what the last part of her story meant.

"Let's have a look at the bottom of your feet," he said surprisingly.

She stared in astonishment at the odd request but swung around obediently, lifting first one foot behind her and then the other.

"That's fine," he breathed. "You had me worried for a while."

"What do you mean?"

"The tracks you left this morning. That Pawnee pattern of your moccasins puzzled me."

She managed to get a half smile on her battered lips. "So that's Pawnee, is it? I made them myself."

He nodded. "Let's get out of here before something else happens. You can tell me the rest of the story on the way to Fort Butler."

He stepped quickly to the trail and whistled for Useless. The girl was at his side promptly, her numbed senses seeming to awaken to what he was planning. "No," she said. "I must not go. I must stay to find my mother."

Somehow Shelby couldn't bring himself to tell her what had happened in Moccasin Valley. The poor kid had been through enough. Better to leave her with

Roscommon County Library Service

WITHDRAWN
FROM STOCK

21

some sort of hope, even if it did lead to future disappointment. "You can't help her here," he told her gently. "The Indians took your mother across the mountains. I saw them take her into their camp. They seemed to be treating her well. The best thing for you is to come along with me to Fort Butler. You can tell your story to the commander there and let the soldiers take charge."

"What do the soldiers care about a miserable foreigner?" she flashed back. "They'll only laugh at me — the way everyone laughed at my father! . . . If we had been treated more decently by your people perhaps we would not have come out here to the . . . free land!"

The bitterness in the last two words surprised Tom. He had forgotten that here was the daughter of the "dumb squarehead". She spoke better English than most people he knew, only a slight broadening of the vowels indicating her alien birth. "Can't say as I blame you for feeling that way," he told her. "I was what they called a galvanized Yankee so I know what it's like to be kicked around by everybody else. Just the same you'd better head for the fort. There's no point in hangin' around here unless you want to find yourself keepin' house for some stinkin' buck in a tepee full of fleas."

Too late he remembered that the girl's mother had been made captive and he was sorry for the remark. However, she didn't seem to be concerned with that part of it. Her decision seemed to be a matter of calm thought and Shelby felt a sense of relief. At any rate he was not going to be bothered by a woman's hysterics.

"I'll go," she said finally — "unless I will be a burden to you."

"That's neither here nor there. If I can make it I can take you — but don't get your hopes too high. If this Indian uprising is as bad as it seems we may never get out of this valley."

Useless slogged up and nibbled patiently at his master's sleeve. Karen stared wonderingly at the three horses and turned gravely to Shelby. "How long have you been on the trail?" she asked abruptly.

"Since daylight yesterday — all except a couple of hours last night when I was watchin' the Indian village. The ponies are kinda fagged, I reckon."

"That second horse is ready to drop!" she snapped. "You certainly can't hope to make any kind of a run for safety with animals like that!"

"I'm glad you understand," he said dryly, scratching his whiskers in some embarrassment. "I was so set on gettin' you outa this valley that I neglected this part of it. Carried away by my own arguments, I guess."

She smiled thinly. "You mean you are willing to risk everything to get me to safety. I won't go." There was no tension in the words, only a calm statement of the facts. It struck Shelby that this girl was a pretty cool customer.

He grinned a little, then stepped forward and seized her bodily, lifting her to the saddle even as she voiced a hasty protest. "No arguments, Sis," he said. "We're goin' out together or we don't go at all. You wouldn't make me stick around here to be killed, would you?"

She looked down at him strangely. "You're crazy," she said, a touch of wonder in her tone — "and very kind. Well, let's go. Maybe I can be of some help."

Something in the tilt of her battered chin gave him a moment of confidence and he turned to lead the way down the trail, his gun still in his hand.

They covered a quarter mile in complete silence. Then Karen spoke softly but with decision. "We will leave the trail here. Steady that second horse, will you; he's in pretty bad shape."

Shelby grinned at her calm assumption of leadership but dropped back obediently. "It's your party, Sis," he said. "If you've got any smart ideas now's the time to trot 'em out." It seemed strange to let her take over the direction of affairs but she seemed to know what she was doing — and anyway he was too tired to think.

She swung Useless from the trail, heading toward the slash where White Water Creek was disgracing its name with a tumbled flood of yellow. There didn't seem to be any ford there nor any sign of a trail on the opposite bank but she headed directly into the stream. "It is not deep," she called back, "but the rocks will be slippery. Don't let that horse fall down!"

"I'll support him if he'll support me," Shelby told her with a rueful laugh. "I hope you know what you're doing, though. I'd hate to get all wet for nothing."

She flashed him a half smile, appreciating the irony of it. After all, she had been soaking wet just as long as he had. She urged Useless upstream until the rear horse was in the creek, then she turned abruptly and doubled

24

on her tracks. "If anyone trails us it will look like we went up the creek," she explained briefly.

Shelby didn't reply. She seemed to know what she was doing and that was enough for him. He was having all he could do to keep his footing on the slippery stones of the creek bottom. Cramps brought on by the icy water stabbed at his legs but he waded on, keeping a firm grip on the pack pony's bridle until they had progressed nearly two hundred yards downstream. There a little brook rushed in from the same side on which they had previously been traveling and Karen headed her cavalcade into it, quickly passing the well-defined valley trail.

Tom began to appreciate her strategy. To have entered the brook directly from the trail would have made it too easy for trackers. This way there was nothing to indicate any progress along the brook. For a squarehead this kid wasn't so dumb.

They followed the rivulet for another quarter mile, coming to where the water dashed down across a series of sloping ledges. "We go up," she said. "I think the horses can make it if we help."

Her voice carried a ring of triumph and Shelby was left to wonder as she slid from the saddle and motioned for him to lead the way. Odd sort of a ragamuffin. She had been unwilling to make a burden of herself but now that she had established herself as a partner she was pretty cocky. Maybe she was lucky to be that way. It kept her mind from the horrors she had seen.

"How much further?" he asked.

"Not far. We'll stop and rest as soon as we're safe."

"Then we'd better take the broncs up this rock one at a time."

She nodded and went to work on a knot. "You take the saddle horse and I'll stay here with the others until you come back. There's a little glade just ahead and I don't think anyone will ever find us there. It's well concealed and we'll be as safe there as anywhere. The horses must have rest."

He grinned down at her before starting Useless up the sloping ledge. "Sis, you're all right. I thought my luck had petered out but I reckon I hit pay dirt again when I run across you. Lucky I decided to let you help me."

"Stop talking and hurry," she snapped. "I'm cold."

"Yes, ma'am," he said meekly.

The glade was everything she had promised, a towering overhang of rock hiding it from any observer above while the forest closed it in on all sides. The sound of a waterfall close at hand indicated that the brook had its source in some niche of the rocks so there would be no chance of an intruder coming downstream.

Tom left Useless trembling in a little patch of sunlight and returned to help with the pack animals. It was slippery work getting them up the rocks but the job was finally successful. When the last horse was led into the glade Karen went down in a heap but Tom paid her scant attention. "Take it easy," he said, and went to work at the job of unpacking the ponies.

"Slave driver!" she said, getting up to unsaddle Useless.

He grinned. "Had to do it right away," he explained. "The broncs need the relief and I had to get at it before I let myself remember how tired I am. You've done your share. I'll handle the rest of this."

She ignored him and went on with what she was doing. He chuckled dryly. "There's some grub in that left hand saddle bag. Better get it out. We'll need it."

"You're really a lifesaver," she told him. "I was wondering if I would ever see food again."

"That's just my part of the deal," he chuckled. "You supply the room. I supply the board. Nice cozy little arrangement we have."

Something in her silence made him look up. She was staring at him in sudden alarm. It puzzled him for a moment, then he laughed. "Don't get spooked up, Sis," he said. "I'm too tired to be dangerous." Trust a woman to get ideas the minute she had a breathing spell! The kid was suddenly scared at finding herself alone in the hills with him — and it wouldn't do a bit of good to remind her that she had about as much girlish charm as the briar patch she had been through.

CHAPTER
FOUR

The morning sun was cutting broad diagonal stripes through the tops of the pines by the time they had eaten the strips of jerked antelope meat which Karen had handed out. Tom chuckled but made no comment at the way the girl had taken charge. Her character seemed to be a peculiar mixture of efficiency and feminine inconsistency. She had risen nobly to the emergency but now she was worried over a trifle. With a crushing burden of real trouble to carry she had found time to fret over her unconventional situation.

He wondered at her background, recalling the air of triumph which she had shown on arriving here at the glen. Maybe she was just happy at having been of service but it was possible that this was just a device for keeping him here in the valley. Perhaps she had played up to his weariness in order to get her way. He swallowed the last mouthful of meat and climbed painfully to his feet. If that was her plan there was no need to interfere — yet. Later he might have to take measures to enforce her retreat from the valley but for the present he was thankful for the refuge.

He grunted as he moved toward the packs. Those leg cramps which had seized him in the creek had left sharp aches in his muscles and the brief rest had been enough to bring the stiffness.

Karen looked up in alarm at his exclamation. He explained, grinning to hide the pain. "Knots in my legs," he said shortly. "I reckon I was too tired to take that ice water treatment."

Slipping off the rawhide thongs which bound the pelts he began to sort through them, hunting for any dry ones which might be in the middles of the bales. Now that the tension was relieved he was ready to drop from exhaustion but he also knew that he didn't dare lie down to sleep in his wet garments. Those leg cramps would have partners all over his body if he tried to sleep like this.

When he had found enough dry pelts to serve as a protection against the wet ground he unrolled his blankets from the protecting poncho, thankful that he had left the roll intact during the night.

He peeled off the buckskin shirt as the girl eyed him doubtfully. Wringing the water out of it he hung it over a bush and turned to pick up one of the blankets. "That other blanket is yours, Sis," he said easily — "if you're not too fussy about it being kinda ripe and flavored with old age. Better rub yourself down good and roll up in it. Help yourself to the driest pelts you can find. We can't have you catching cold."

He turned abruptly and walked down toward a spot where bushes lined the brook. There he washed the mud from his moccasins and leggings, stripping himself of every clammy garment. When each piece was thoroughly rinsed he rubbed himself hard until he was dry, then wrapped the blanket about him and returned to the glade.

Karen had taken the hint and disappeared at the far side of the glen. In a few minutes she also returned and spread her clothing in the sun to dry. Tom noted that beyond the ragged buffalo cape there was precious little to her wardrobe. Buckskin breeches such as a squaw might wear, shapeless undergarments, moccasins and a crudely beaded jacket seemed to be the sum total of her outfit — if he could assume that she now wore nothing but the blanket which wrapped her from neck to ankle.

She met his glance squarely. "Stretch out there on the furs," she ordered briskly — "face down. I'll see if I can't rub some of those cramps out of your legs."

He grinned and spread himself as ordered. "You amaze me, Sis," he said over his shoulder. "For a gal with such an ugly black eye you sure have got a heart of gold. Even among my best friends I wouldn't get a treatment like this . . . Mainly because I haven't any friends."

"Probably because you talk too much," she told him severely. "Turn your face around there and keep it turned. I haven't any way to hold this blanket up."

"Yes, ma'am," he murmured. Might as well let the poor kid think she was being daring. She was trying hard to help and it wasn't her fault that she wasn't the type to get a man excited.

It was nearly dusk when he awoke, to find the girl already dressed and moving about. "Hello there," he greeted. "You didn't sleep long."

30

"I went up the side of the ridge to look around," she told him, pointing to where a slope wound around the north edge of the overhang. "I wanted to see what the valley looked like from here."

Tom realized that from above she could look down upon the heap of ashes which had been her home. He wondered if she was still planning to remain in the valley instead of hunting safety. If so, he would have to tell her about her mother. "Any sign of any savages?" he asked quietly.

"No. Everything seems very quiet. I think we can ride out with some degree of safety."

He saw that she was working at a bundle of furs, already having one pack tied up. Apparently she wasn't expecting to delay any longer — if she had had any such desire in the first place. Certainly she had recognized the pressing need for resting the horses, so perhaps her motive had been the same as his own all the time.

She turned her back significantly as he made no move to climb out of the blankets. "Time to get up," she told him.

Shelby chuckled and reached for his pants. She was a cool hand, all right. It struck him that at any other time he might have resented having a girl give orders like this but somehow he didn't feel at all irritated by it now. So far her judgment had been good and he felt content to let her have her own way. It was certainly better than having her crying about her parents.

He studied her profile slyly as she worked over the pelts. Maybe she wasn't such a homely little squarehead after all. That black eye had twisted her face all out of shape but the one good eye was a clear blue which went well with the gold of her hair. Maybe the face wouldn't be so bad if it had half a chance.

He was dressed in time to help with the last bale of pelts, turning immediately to the business of getting the pack horses loaded. None of the animals seemed any the worse for their ordeal and Shelby quickly had one of them rigged out with his valuable load. As he turned to repeat the performance with the other horse he found to his surprise that Karen had already adjusted the pack saddle and was boosting the heavy bales into place. He sprang to her aid but she went on with the job, throwing the hitch as though she had done it many times before.

"Good job," he approved. "How'd you learn to be so good at that kind of work?"

"My father knew many things," she said quietly. "He tried to teach me the things I should know in order that I could help him with our ranch."

He turned away in sudden embarrassment and called Useless. Once again he had gone out of his way to remind the girl of her loss. Pretty soon he ought to learn to keep his big mouth shut and let her alone. It would be little enough pay for the help she had been in getting him the rest he needed so badly.

"Don't feel sorry," she said, reading his thoughts. "We can't take time for that . . . Is there any place where we can find help nearer than Fort Butler? It will take us so long to go there."

"Nothing closer that will do us any good," he replied. "The Overland Stage route runs within fifteen miles or so but it would never do to head that way."

"Why not?"

He knelt to place his hand on the ground, fingers slightly spread. "Here's a map of this country. The foothills stretch out into the plains like fingers. Fort Butler lies at the tip of my third finger and the stage line runs up the valley between my third and little fingers."

She laughed shortly at his literal description but nodded her understanding. He went on, "We're right in here somewhere between my first and middle fingers. To reach the stage line we would have to go back over the ridge I crossed last night, wade through a pack of ornery Indians and then scale another finger that's mostly rocks with no trail across it. My guess is that our only chance is to take the long way and head for Butler. If we make it we're pretty sure to find help while if we risk the cross-country jaunt we'll likely find nothing at the end but a burned stage station. The Cheyennes won't have missed a chance to raid the stage line if there's a real war on."

"I understand. You're the boss now so we'll do whatever you say. My term as guide is over now that we've had some rest."

"Thanks. Then suppose you trot out the rest of that meat and we'll get on our way."

"No more meat now," she said decidedly. "You're the general but I'm running the commissary. We're saving that scrap of food until we see how badly we're going to need it. Pull up your belt another notch and let's go."

"Commissary, eh?" he grunted. "You talk more like a drill sergeant." He studied her closely for a moment. "I'll bet you're a right nice-lookin' girl when you get your face in good working order," he chuckled. "No woman ever bossed a man so natural-like unless she was pretty sure of havin' him obey orders — and it's usually the pretty ones that can get away with it. I'm curious to see what you'll look like when some of the hide grows back on."

A blush broke out among the bruises but she managed a quick retort. "You're no blushing violet yourself, trapper. I expect you must be quite a beau when you come out from behind those whiskers. Now let's stop talking foolishness and get started."

He turned without a reply and headed down the brook, scouting carefully before returning to work the horses down over the shelving ledge. They reached the valley trail without mishap, taking up a brisk march to the southeast when it became apparent that the trail had been untraveled during the day. There was a brief delay as the girl tried to argue against riding but Shelby didn't permit that to last long. With a quick sweep of his arm he lifted her and set her behind him. "Old Useless can carry double for a while, 'specially when the extra load is no bigger than you. After a while we'll take turns walking when the trail's clear."

"I'm not so little," she retorted, hooking her fingers in his belt. "Stop talking to me as though I were a child!"

34

"All right, grandmaw," he laughed. "No offense meant. Maybe you're not so big but you pull a lot for your weight." He recalled her effort to lift the bales of furs, wondering that she had been able to do it. For a little woman she seemed to have plenty of power — and she wasn't keen on having him forget the fact!

Darkness closed down almost immediately but the trail was easy even in the gloom. Tom was pretty sure of his ground now, even though White Water Valley was new to him. He saw that they were passing through the same sort of a valley as he had his eye on for his ranch. Apparently the White Water and the Moccasin were twins, running parallel for another twenty-odd miles before they joined, a single spur of ridge — third finger — sticking out into the plains toward Fort Butler.

They traveled rapidly but without forcing the pace, stopping from time to time to rest the horses. In case of emergency Tom wanted his animals to have something in reserve. No signs of pursuit had come to bother them but that was no guarantee that they wouldn't strike other war parties somewhere ahead.

Conversation was meagre except when they were stopped for rests and then they merely exchanged remarks on the progress of the flight. Something had made the girl strangely reticent and Tom suspected that she had withdrawn into her shell as a result of that little flurry of banter which had marked the start of the trip. Both of them had let down the bars a little then and now they were trying to put them back up again. It was better that way under the circumstances.

When the trail permitted, Shelby walked, trying to save Useless as much as possible. It was at these times that Karen seemed most disposed to talk, reaching out with her voice in the darkness toward the man she could no longer touch. She was trying desperately to hold up under the emotional tension and Tom fashioned his replies with that fact in mind. He had to keep her spirits up. He couldn't afford to let her become emotional.

At dawn they were in country where the foothills were dwindling into the Great Plains. Just ahead lay the junction of the White Water and the Moccasin — while nearly twenty-five miles behind them lay the ruin of what had been the home of a family . . . a family that had come into the hills looking for free land. Shelby's jaw tightened at thought of the delusion. What land was ever free? Maybe the settler didn't pay with money and receive a fancy deed but the payment was just as real. Toil, blood and horror. That was the cost of government free land!

Shortly after dawn they made one of their rest stops, picketing the animals in a patch of woods while Tom made a vain attempt to find something eatable in the woodland. No more food was in the deerskin bag and he didn't dare risk a shot at game. It was a case of find edible roots or go hungry.

"Sorry," he said when he returned to where Karen waited with the horses. "No cream for the coffee today. Shall I complain to the manager?"

She shrugged a little. "I'm not hungry anyway."

He realized that she was telling the truth. For a day and a half now she had been keeping her emotions in check. It was no wonder she had lost her appetite.

He wondered fleetingly what he would do if she should crack under the strain. That would be almost as bad as running into more Indians. His thoughts were interrupted by her sudden question.

"What did you mean yesterday when you said you were a galvanized Yankee?"

The unexpectedness of the question made him laugh aloud. It was a sore spot with him but he was glad to talk about it now, anything to keep the topic away from the present troubles.

"I'm a Texan," he explained. "Cowpuncher by trade. When Texas seceded I joined up with a cavalry outfit and found myself eatin' hog and hominy in Johnston's army. I was around just long enough to get a corporal's stripes and then I had the bad judgment to get captured by the Yanks.

"A year in Rock Island prison was about all I could stomach so I took what looked like the easy way out. The Yanks offered to release any of us Rebs who would volunteer for service against the Indians, guaranteeing us that we wouldn't be sent against the Confederacy. I jumped at the chance."

"Is that what you mean by a galvanized Yankee?"

"Yep. I understand that wasn't the original meaning, but that's what they called us."

"And what made you think such a past would make you capable of understanding my case? Surely there was no particular shame attached to that. Not like the crime of being a foreigner!"

Her bitterness disturbed him — and he couldn't understand why. Probably she had reason to feel the way she did, and surely he had his own grievances, but she put him on the defensive just the same.

"You don't know the half of it," he told her. "The other Yanks didn't trust us and the officers handled us like they would a chain gang. It wasn't long until I was sorry I hadn't stayed in the calaboose."

"But that's all over now," she pointed out. "Surely you're not bothered by it any more."

He laughed shortly. "The war didn't end it. When my enlistment expired I went home. Nobody would have anything to do with a man who had changed his coat — and anyway the damned Carpetbaggers had stolen everything my folks had ever owned. I came back out here. I thought the Indians were at least honest."

He jumped up hurriedly, aware that he had led the conversation directly back to the sore subject of Indian treachery.

"Time to move," he blurted. "Cryin' on your shoulder won't be no help to either of us."

She smiled faintly, more in appreciation of his effort to divert her than anything else. The sun was rising high as they pushed around more to the south, both of them now walking as the horses showed signs of fatigue. No longer did they have the protection of either the hills or darkness. If war parties were scouting the edge of the plains they would be pretty much at the mercy of attackers.

They pushed doggedly ahead for nearly an hour. Then at the crest of a rise dead ahead three mounted warriors appeared.

Tom swore softly and stopped in his tracks. "Sioux!" he exclaimed, mechanically passing his hand across his throat in the sign for the tribe. "Cutthroats mean trouble. Get the horses back into that stand of trees. I reckon we're in for it!"

He jerked his Colt from its holster and spun the cylinder, quickly adjusting a cap to the chamber which he carried loaded but unprimed under the hammer. "Know how to shoot a gun like this?" he asked as he worked.

"Not just like that," she said. "Tell me."

"Not much to tell. Six shots just as fast as you can thumb back the hammer and pull the trigger. It's a new model and a good one. Don't waste any shots — and save the last one in case things get hopeless."

She nodded silently and let her slender fingers close over the heavy butt.

"Get going!" he snapped. "The red brethren are getting ready to charge!"

CHAPTER
FIVE

Karen turned Useless toward the timber. As Shelby ran alongside, pulling his carbine from the boot, he could see that her lips had drawn tight. There was fear in her eyes but the lips showed nothing but grim anger.

"Take the ponies plenty deep," he ordered. "It won't be any protection against bullets but it'll keep the devils from stampeding them. That's what they usually try to do."

She nodded her understanding, then lowered her head doggedly as she sent Useless crashing into the brush. She wasn't much to look at, Shelby thought, but she made a good ally when the going got bad.

He took up his position behind the biggest tree he could find, checking the carbine as he did so. Maybe this would be the end of the trail but he determined to make the Sioux pay full price. There was only a moment of brief regret as he recalled the fine plans which had fallen apart so quickly, then he became completely concerned with the immediate problem of living.

The warriors came on with a rush, drumming their heels against the flanks of their ponies and yelling wildly at sight of unexpected prey. Tom felt a momentary flash of relief that no more warriors had appeared but he knew that it was too early for optimism. Maybe these fellows were simply scouts coming back from Butler — but they might be part of a large party.

Already the leading Sioux was firing as he rode, using the regular Indian plan of trying to panic the enemy. Apparently he was armed with some sort of repeating rifle so Tom picked him as his first target. Better get rid of the best armed enemy first.

He knelt quietly, lining his sights on the savage but waiting until he was sure of a hit. This was no time for a miss, even though the Spencer carbine would allow him seven quick shots. It was hard to hold his fire with the target before him but five years on the plains had taught him something of Indian warfare. A plains Indian was a fierce fighter while he was riding in the breakneck speed of the chase but something in the savage mind seemed baffled by an enemy who refused to be chased. That was one reason why so many small bodies of troops had won fights with superior numbers of Indians.

Now Shelby determined to wait until the last moment, hopeful of shaking the raiders' nerves.

The Spencer's front sight held steadily on the painted face which loomed above the foremost pinto's ears. When the Sioux were almost upon him Tom squeezed the trigger firmly and a sharp crack opened the defense. The leading warrior went back over his pony's rump as though he had been hit by a club, the fifty-six caliber slug doing fearful execution at short range like that.

Tom worked the trigger-guard action and took swift aim at the second Oglala. Just as he pulled the trigger the Indian wheeled his horse and swung to the left, the move saving his life. Tom swore aloud at the miss and jerked at the mechanism again. To his dismay the weapon jammed.

Fortunately, the attackers had swung off in a circle, declining to come on into the trees against that fire. Tom worked feverishly at the jammed gun, cursing himself for the accident. Only last fall he had passed up an opportunity to trade the carbine for one of the new model Spencers with the improved cut-off. Now he was threatened with disaster because of a known flaw in the older weapon.

He jerked his hunting knife out in an instant, probing anxiously at the jammed cartridge.

The two remaining Oglalas were coming back now, the circling operation having fired them with new valor. This time they would come on in . . . and still the carbine refused to function.

Tom swung his head a little to call back to Karen. "Go on back into the timber. Cut the pack horses loose. Get on Useless and run for it!"

Apparently the girl didn't understand. At any rate she didn't obey. He could hear her crashing through the brush behind him, coming closer to the spot which would shortly be the scene of a finish fight. A bullet clipped the boughs above his head as one of the Indians tried a shot.

"Get back!" Shelby yelled again, not taking time to look behind him. "Don't be a fool! Get on that horse and ride!"

He made one last frantic gouge with his knife, his mind in a whirl from trying to think of so many things at once. The screeching Sioux were almost into the edge of the woods and Karen was still coming on from the rear.

Then everything seemed to happen in one riotous moment. The jammed cartridge slid into the chamber and he snapped the breechblock into place. The two Indians drove their plunging ponies straight into the brush. He had a glimpse of a lance coming down at him, then he fired squarely into a painted face. At the same instant an explosion boomed in his ear.

As though through a mist he saw his man go down. He swung the carbine toward the other savage, pumping in a fresh cartridge as he moved the weapon. The action was purely mechanical for there was no need of another shot. That blast in his ear had come from his own six-gun in the hand of Karen Neilson. Both warriors were sprawling on the ground, one already dead while the other was giving vent to a last gurgling scream.

Tom didn't stop to voice the words which flashed into his mind. He jumped for the rawhide hackamore of the nearer pony, pulling the pinto down under control before the animal could get himself clear of the underbrush. Only then did he turn to stare wonderingly at the yellow-haired girl who stood over a dead warrior, the Army Model Colt still smoking in her hand.

He let out his breath in a heavy grunt. "You'll do, Sis," he approved. "For a gal with fancy schooling you sure pick things up fast. Thanks for the help. I thought for a minute I was going to be just another coup on a redskin's brag list."

She didn't look up as he spoke but stood there staring down at the dead Oglala, her battered lips murmuring something he was unable to catch. He couldn't decide whether she was sick at the thought of having killed the Indian or whether she was thinking in terms of revenge. Certainly there would have been ample reason for the latter.

He took the Colt from her unresisting fingers. "I'll take care of this now," he said gently. "A .44 is a lot of hardware for a paw the size of yours. Besides, I think maybe we can find a better weapon for you. Unless that first buck smashed it when he took his dive there's a good repeating rifle out there."

She seemed to pay no attention and he spoke more crisply, anxious to get her mind away from the scene. This was no time to let her get into any hysterics! "Get the ponies! Hurry now while I look around and see if these devils had anything worth taking. We might even be lucky enough to find some jerked meat in their saddle bags."

She looked up as though startled, then nodded and faded back into the timber without a word. He watched to assure himself that her step was firm and that she wasn't going to faint or do anything else of that nature. Then he moved out cautiously into the open, watching in all directions for any new hostiles. They had beaten

44

off one attack successfully enough but it was a fair bet that the firing would have attracted the attention of other warriors.

It didn't take long to discover that none of the Indians had been carrying equipment worth taking — with the exception of the brave who had sported the repeater. The rifle was a brand-new Henry, in excellent condition and with a good supply of cartridges. Shelby picked it up and strode back toward the timber just in time to meet Karen as she came out with the horses.

Tom swung to the back of the captured pinto. "You ride Useless," he directed. "He's gentle — and maybe has better manners than his boss. I'll fork this pinto 'til I see how wild he is. After that he's your hoss."

He ranged himself beside her as she rode out into the open, handing over the Henry. "Full equipment now, partner," he grinned. "With a gun and a horse apiece we ought to make a heap of trouble for the next gang that tries to get gay with us. Sorry, but I didn't locate any grub."

She took the rifle, still silent, and looked at it without seeming to know just what she was doing. Once more Tom had the fear of hysteria come over him. Fighting Indians wasn't so bad but he didn't want to have any hysterical girl on his hands.

Hastily he began to show her the operation of the Henry's lever action, talking rapidly as he did so. "You just keep pumping this lever to throw the cartridges in and pulling the trigger to throw 'em out — through the muzzle. Just feel the balance of it! Better rifle than anything the government issues to the army. Beats all how the Indians can get 'em! Here's some cartridges. Magazine's already full. Fifteen shots in a hurry. It don't pack the wallop of this Spencer but I'll bet it won't give you gray hairs like this thing did to me. Tuck it in the saddle boot but be ready to grab it."

She nodded silently, still unwilling to trust herself with words, and followed Tom along the edge of the woodland. For upwards of a mile they kept to the timber edge, ready to take refuge in case of further attacks. Then the forest dropped away and they headed out into the open, bracing themselves for the last stage of the journey, the open country near Fort Butler. Tom hoped it wouldn't be a race: the horses were in no condition to stand it.

Neither of them said a word until they were well away from the timbered hills. Then Karen swung in her saddle, looking back at the valley they had left. "I'll be back," she said softly.

Shelby watched her without asking any questions. He thought she was making a promise to her mother but she quickly set him right on that matter.

"My father wanted a home back there," she said soberly. "We planned to have cattle in the valleys and enough grain and other crops for our own use. He thought it was a fine spot for people who wanted nothing but to be let alone. I'm going to carry out those plans if it's the last thing I ever do in this world!"

Tom merely nodded. It didn't occur to him that he was seeing a new side to her character, something deeper than he had seen before. The vow was so like his own thoughts that he considered it a mere matter of course. "My plans are something like that," he told her. "I have a spot all picked out in Moccasin Valley. When we get the Indians chased out we'll be neighbors — if we live that long."

Her mood seemed to change abruptly. Meeting his glance, a half smile on her battered lips, she asked, "Why did you say I was all right for a girl with an education?"

He chuckled a little. It was the same sort of question she had asked before, going back to an almost forgotten remark. "Gosh, Sis," he laughed, "it ain't safe to say anything to you. A man never knows when you'll come back and ask about it."

"My name is Karen — not Sis," she reminded him. "Why did you say it?"

"I don't know. I say a lot of things that I don't figure out ahead of time. However, it's easy to see that you did get a good education. You talk like it — even though I'll bet you didn't learn English in this country."

"Correct. I went to school in both Denmark and England. My father taught me English."

"Denmark? I thought you folks were Swedes."

"You would! Everybody called Father a Swede — or a squarehead! We were just miserable foreigners to you people!"

He flinched before the bitterness in her voice but tried to pass it off with a laugh. "Don't blame me, Sis — I mean Karen. It's no insult to call you a Swede and anyway I wouldn't poke fun at anybody. I'm a pariah myself, remember."

He studied her with a puzzled frown before asking, "How did it happen that folks like yours should come over here to live in the wilderness?"

She didn't reply for some moments, then she spoke without looking toward him. "Maybe I'm something like you. We came here because we didn't have anywhere else to go. My father was a man of some standing in Denmark. We lived happily and I thought the world was a pretty easy place. Then the Prussians swept through the country and we had to leave. My father had been an outspoken critic of Bismarck's schemes so it wasn't safe for him to stay in Schleswig with the Prussians in full control. We came to America because we had heard it was the land of real opportunity."

Her lips drew into a tight little line. "A country of free people and free land — where everyone sneered at us and where my father paid for his free land with his life!"

Again Shelby found himself on the defensive. In spite of the fact that his own life had been scarcely less bitter he wanted to protest against this indictment. "Plenty of men have paid for free land that way," he said finally. "It's the chance we all have to take. The free things often cost the most — but maybe that's the important point. That and the freedom that goes with them."

"That's why I'm going back to the valley," she said simply.

CHAPTER
SIX

It was late afternoon when they approached the cluster of low buildings which Shelby knew as Fort Butler. The place hadn't changed any during the winter. It was still a neglected military post, the government buildings just as crude as the three civilian structures which kept them company.

The fort itself consisted of a long frame barracks facing a row of slab houses which masqueraded as Officers' Row. Quartermasters' sheds and a storehouse completed the third side of the quadrangle while the fourth remained open, facing the rear of the stage station, the trading post and a solitary abandoned cabin. A sizeable corral had been erected across the trail from the stage station while the government corrals and stables were at the far side of the army post behind the Quartermaster's shed.

The whole scene had an air of neglect and for some moments Shelby wondered if the post had been abandoned. He realized that an Indian raid would have been marked by the burning of buildings but it was difficult for him to put aside his dread. The experiences of the past few days had led him to expect almost anything so long as it was bad. It wasn't until the afternoon sun gleamed on the blue of a sentry's jacket that he felt any sense of security.

The post was guarded, all right, but not by a force of any size. Either the garrison was out campaigning or the post had been left under a skeleton crew. Probably the latter, judging by the neglected appearance of the buildings. Only the trading post showed any signs of care, the stage company station crumbling into ruins for lack of repair. With the rumors of the railroad coming on through, it wasn't likely that the stage company would be spending any money to repair holdings that would soon be discarded.

They rode in silence toward the trading post, passed a couple of grinning troopers at the end of the barracks and suddenly found themselves between buildings at last. Only then did Shelby speak the relief he felt. With so many things happening he hadn't even wanted to hope for much until making certain that Fort Butler was in friendly hands.

"Well," he remarked with elaborate casualness, "we finally made it. If I ever need to make another tour through hostile country I'll know where to look for a mighty good partner."

She smiled only faintly at the compliment. "Now we must find Lieutenant Brannigan and see what can be done to rescue my mother. I met the lieutenant last summer and I feel sure he will do everything possible." Her voice was tense now and Shelby groaned silently. It wasn't going to be any easier to tell her now than it would have been out there in the hills. Still, he couldn't put it off any longer. Too many things might happen to . . .

"There's an officer!" she said suddenly. "Over there by one of those little cabins. Shall I go tell him?"

Four men stood together at the far side of the parade ground, one of them wearing the uniform of a captain. The others were clad in nondescript plains garments, two of them particularly looking the part of scouts. The other seemed more carefully dressed, more like a tenderfoot, but he wasn't the one who took Shelby's eye. Something about the big scout had brought a sense of unpleasant recognition to Tom's mind and in his sudden doubt he almost let Karen ride away.

"Better wait until I leave these pelts with Dutchy Schwartz," he said quietly. "There's something I want to talk to you about before you report to the authorities."

She flashed him a glance of curiosity and surprise but offered no objection. They continued in silence to the door of the trading post where a roly-poly little man had come out to greet them.

"Halloo, drapper!" Schwartz grunted, the words cheery for all the effort it seemed to require to say them. "It looks like it was a goot vinter, hein?"

Shelby laughed aloud. "Schwartz," he said critically, "you're fatter than ever! I hope honesty goes with the weight. I want a better price on my pelts than you gave me last year."

Schwartz grinned in delight. "Tom Shelby, py golly! I don't know you midt der viskers. Come in und pring der lady."

"I'd appreciate it if you'd take care of Miss Neilson, Dutchy, but I've got to go over and talk to the commander. The Cheyennes are on the warpath."

Behind him Karen gave a sudden exclamation of alarm. "Tom! Look out! He's going to shoot you!"

Shelby didn't wait to ask questions. With one twisting slide he was out of the saddle, his six-gun in his hand. From the corner of the building a gun crashed, its slug tearing a big hole in the air directly above the pinto's blanket saddle. Shelby snapped a return shot at the corner, then a pair of troopers came running.

From behind the building a voice yelled, "It's Brewster, the stage bandit! Better shoot first and look later!"

One of the troopers seemed about to take the advice but Tom raised his voice hurriedly. "Don't shoot so quick, soldier! That polecat's lyin'." He stepped out from behind the pony, deliberately exposing himself to the oncoming troopers even as he watched for any sign of another shot from the building.

The other trooper seemed to take in the situation. "All right, Pew," he said to the unseen bushwhacker. "We'll take charge now. What's up?"

The voice rasped again. "That gent is Brewster, the outlaw what robbed the stage at Box Elder and then killed the trapper next day. We tried to get him."

"He's a liar," Shelby said quietly. "Schwartz knows who I am. You don't need to do any shooting. I'm willing to talk peaceable — but I won't sit around while any lousy sidewinders take pot shots at my back!"

Either his tone or the presence of the troopers seemed to give his assailants courage. Two men stepped out from behind the house, one of them a ratty little fellow of middle age while the other was about Shelby's age and size. The big man seemed familiar and Tom realized that it was the same fellow he had seen with the officer. In fact, the little man had also been one of the quartet.

It was the little man who spoke. "Captain Bonsall ordered us to take him," he snarled. "Dead or alive."

"I'm takin' orders from Lieutenant Brannigan," the trooper snapped. "If there's any arrestin' to be done on this post the guard'll do it!"

Shelby grinned and slipped his gun back into its holster. "Thanks, trooper," he said. "All I want is a chance to prove who I am."

The man grinned. "Come on, then. We'll let you talk to the lieutenant."

Shelby nodded and turned to speak with the gaping Schwartz. "Take care of my stuff, Dutchy. Get Mom Schwartz to look after the girl. I'll stand good for anything."

The move had placed his back squarely to the ratty man. Suddenly a gun jabbed into his back and the little man snarled, "Get 'em up. I'll drill you if you or these tin soldiers make a wrong move. You're goin' to see Cap Bonsall — with or without holes in your hide!"

Something in the man's tone warned Shelby that they wanted him dead much more than they wanted him alive. The little man was deliberately setting up a situation where he might have an excuse to commit the murder he had previously failed to accomplish. One little move and the rat-faced man would shoot.

Tom raised his hands slowly, twisting his head as he did so. He didn't intend to be shot down without a fight but he moved slowly, trying to puzzle out the odd situation before making his play. "What's all the fuss?" he asked mildly. "I didn't —"

"Shut up!" The little man jabbed his gun harder under Tom's shoulder blade. The other scout was standing back grinning but his hand was not far from his gun.

Suddenly Tom knew the big fellow. Not that it helped, merely telling him how dangerous a spot he was in. The big man was a border desperado named Hogan, known throughout eastern Kansas as Grinner. The man had no trace of moral scruples but his ever present good humor deceived many people — to their subsequent dismay. He used his smile to cover his thoughts and intentions just as a highwayman might have used a mask. If Hogan had a fist in this deal it wasn't going to be safe or pleasant.

Shelby realized that the two troopers were his best bet although just now both of them were caught foul. Neither dared make a move for fear their prisoner would be killed by the runty scout. Tom knew he would have to make his own break and depend on the troopers to step in.

Forcing a grin he spoke again, twisting his head to look around over his right shoulder. "You ain't foolin', are you, gents?" he asked. "This ain't the most

54

comfortable position for a man's hands and I ain't in the mood —"

The complaining speech broke off as the little man opened his toothless mouth to snarl a reply. In the proper split second of distraction Shelby made his play. His right elbow had swung back a little as he turned his head, now it came down sharply to knock the little man's gun aside. In the same motion of his body Tom brought his left hand around in a sweeping blow that landed under the scout's ear.

The little man went down like a poleaxed bull but Shelby didn't rest on his quick laurels. Hogan was still to be accounted for. The trapper's right hand went on down as he twisted and before the little man hit the ground Shelby had his own gun in his hand, its muzzle covering Hogan.

Both troopers lifted their carbines hesitantly but Tom included them both in a friendly grin as Hogan swore. He nodded toward the two scouts, his glance on the taller trooper.

"Better gather up their guns while I keep 'em on good behavior. After they're disarmed I'll let you have mine. I'll be peaceful enough if I'm going to get treated right but I ain't keen on getting shot in the back by a miserable polecat."

The lanky soldier stepped forward, picking up the fallen gun before he moved over cautiously to take Hogan's. Tom watched narrowly but for all his care he was still conscious of the gathering audience. In the swift flurry of events Karen Neilson had remained motionless on the steps of the trading post, her eyes wide as she heard Shelby denounced as a bandit and killer. Horror, anger and finally disbelief showed on her bruised features and Tom realized hopefully that she was trying to trust him. He didn't exactly know why it made any difference to him that she should feel that way about him — but somehow it did.

He lowered his gun as the tall trooper moved back with Hogan's .44. "Pleasant reception you boys give callers," he remarked. "Now let's go see what this is all about. I've got too much to do to be hanging around while folks mix me up with some road agent."

The troopers grinned thinly and moved in beside him. "Glad to oblige with the reception," the stocky one replied. "We don't hold a party like this for every visitin' outlaw."

Tom winked. "Not many help get themselves locked up, either," he retorted.

He saw that a lanky, rawboned woman had come out on the trading post porch behind Karen. "Hello, Mom," he hailed her. "Take care of the kid, will you? She's had a rough time of it and she's an ace!"

Mrs. Schwartz stared at him dourly but her quirk of a smile belied the rasp in her voice. "Goin' to the jug at last, are ye?" she snapped. "Many's the day I been expectin' it, ye young spalpeen! Hustle along wid yez. A nice gurrl ain't fit to be in the company of such a bewhiskered pirate!"

Shelby grinned. Karen was looking perplexed again but Mom Schwartz would take care of that. Twenty years of married life with Schwartz had sharpened her Irish tongue but it hadn't altered the gold in her heart.

56

He felt a little better for the volley of insults. Mom believed in him or she would never have said a thing like that.

The tall soldier jerked his head toward the open rectangle of the military post. "Come on, stranger. We like your comedy but we can't stick around here all day waitin' fer these two brush apes to jump us again. Remember you're a prisoner and get on your way. Sam! Watch my back in case either of them bandits is hiding out with a gun."

"*Vamos*, brother," Tom agreed, moving away. "Glad to find a couple of honest men around. I didn't know they had any in the army now."

As he swung toward the fort he saw that still another spectator had appeared to watch the proceedings. At the door of the stage station a woman stood in tense silence. She was dressed plainly in a gingham dress but there was nothing else plain about her. Chestnut hair and dark eyes set off the smooth whiteness of her skin while the shapelessness of the dress completely failed to conceal the trimness of her well-rounded figure. She was about the same height as Karen Neilson but with none of the boyish slenderness which made Karen look taller. Her features were almost classic in their perfectly chiseled beauty but now she stood with an intent expression which robbed her features of any life or animation.

"Who's the lady at the remount station?" Tom asked as they swung over toward the parade ground. "She seemed to be glaring at me like I owed her money."

57

"That's Mrs. Elson," the trooper told him gravely. "It was her husband what was shot up at Box Elder a couple of weeks ago. He was the stage driver you . . . er, Brewster killed."

"Oh," Tom said. There didn't seem to be much more worth saying at that point.

It wasn't far to the guardhouse but the distance was ample for Tom to do some heavy thinking. Five minutes ago he had been reasonably well pleased with himself and the world. Now he was caught in some kind of a tight which he couldn't begin to explain. The charge against him might be a simple case of mistaken identity but the rest was not so easy. Who had identified him as Brewster? What kind of a military post was this that there should be such an obvious division of authority? The soldiers seemed to be taking orders from the Lieutenant Brannigan Karen had mentioned but the scouts seemed under the orders of some captain, a higher ranking officer than the lieutenant. It didn't make sense.

What was even more troublesome was the thought of Ed Hogan. What was the big outlaw trying to do? How would the widow of the stage driver react to the arrest of the man believed to be her husband's killer?

He was locked in the guardhouse and left to his own-bitter reflections. Something always happened to him when he ventured into the company of his fellow men. It had been bad enough to be shunned as a turncoat rebel — but now they were fixing to hang him as a bandit and murderer!

58

It seemed like years since he had come down from the trap lines into Moccasin Valley, his mind full of hopeful plans. The outcast years were over. Shelby was about to become a rancher, a stock raiser who would live on peaceful terms with the neighboring Cheyennes. He would become moderately wealthy and perhaps be a power in the country as the territory grew up. He would . . .

Tom snorted aloud at the memory. Fine lot of pipe dreams they had been. It seemed that he was fated to be an outcast all his life. First the Indians had gone hog wild, now the whites were up to their old tricks of making him the goat. If he got himself out of this he'd know better than to try being sociable again!

CHAPTER
SEVEN

The Fort Butler guardhouse was nothing but a log shack. A solid plank door had been fitted into one end and two narrow windows, heavily barred, ventilated the opposite sides. A half dozen wooden benches served as bunks and Shelby dropped wearily on the one under the nearer window. The closing of the heavy door had brought a letdown, an abrupt slackening in the nervous energy which had kept him going during the past two days. Suddenly he knew that he was bone tired. The desperation which had served for energy seemed to leave him with a rush and he could feel nothing but a vast and all powerful weariness.

Still he knew that he couldn't afford to relax now. He had to battle through to some sort of understanding of this new danger which threatened him. He had to know what he was up against before he could hope to find any way out of the mess.

His first problem obviously was to clear himself of that banditry charge . . . but how? He had seen no one since the previous autumn. For all he could prove to the contrary he might have been almost anywhere or done almost anything in the interval. The robbery and murder of Elson had taken place two weeks earlier.

That meant he could hope for no assistance from Karen Neilson. She knew nothing of his movements until some time after the crime was committed. His only hope seemed to be a different attack. He would have to learn who had identified him as Brewster and try to break down that identification.

Meanwhile there was the certainty that Hogan and his runty partner were mighty anxious to get him out of the way. Even more troublesome was the thought of that strikingly handsome Mrs. Elson. A woman like that might be dangerous. She could carry a lot of weight in swaying those in authority. If she chose to be vengeful, blaming Shelby for the death of her husband, she could easily be the most serious danger in the whole dirty business.

The sunset gun boomed and a new guard came on duty outside the door. Shelby paid no attention but a short time later the door bolts rattled and a soldier came in with a plate of food. It was the lanky man who had made the arrest.

"Feed hearty," he invited, putting the food on the bench beside Tom. "There's a hell of a fight on about you but don't let it spoil your appetite."

"Don't worry about my appetite," Shelby laughed. "I haven't had a man-sized bit of grub in about three days. Who's doing the fighting?"

The trooper was already headed for the door but he replied guardedly, "Lieutenant Brannigan and that dam' shorthorn of a captain we've got hanging around. I hope the lieutenant gets his Irish up and tells the polecat where he can go!"

He went out, leaving Tom more bewildered than ever. So the officers were fighting now! Lord! Didn't anybody get along with anybody else around here?

For some minutes he was content to eat, leaving the puzzle until later. Finally, however, when he had cleaned up every scrap and his belly didn't seem quite so hollow, he took thought to his problem again. He could hear the sentry whistling tonelessly by the outside wall so he went to the narrow, barred window and looked out.

The guard was a lanky youth of about Shelby's height but without the solid flesh that made the trapper a big man. He was leaning against the log wall, apparently without a care in the world, his carbine tucked between folded arms. Discipline must be mighty lax around this post, Tom thought, a situation to be expected with the officers at each other's throats and the men gossiping about the fact.

He cleared his throat to attract attention, hopeful of getting the man into conversation. To his surprise the sentry spoke first, quietly and without any appearance of even noticing the prisoner.

"Hello, Reb," he greeted in a languid drawl. "What fer did they fling you in the calaboose? Not that you don't likely deserve it jest on general principles and yore own danged orneriness."

Shelby stared, trying to place that familiar drawling voice and the cut of the bony jaw. "Jeff Speers!" he exclaimed after a moment. "I thought you went back to Alabama when the war was over."

The soldier chuckled audibly. "I did, Reb, but a man cain't git along down there nowadays unless he's willin' to play flunkey fer the dam' Carpetbaggers and Scallywags. My folks was all gone so I traipsed right back out here and 'listed again. I've plumb got over bein' bothered at wearin' a blue jacket — and it's a livin'. What kind o' hell have you been up to now? Hoss thievin'?"

"You tell me!" Tom retorted. "If you're as big a gossip as you used to be you'll know a heap more about it than I do. All I know is that they've got me branded as a jasper name of Brewster. Looks like I'm kinda in a bad spot."

Jeff was expansively confident. "Shucks! I'll tell the lieutenant who you are jest as soon as he gits through with old weasel face."

"Great! I suppose he asks your talented advice about everything! And who is your friend weasel face?"

"Cap'n Bonsall. He come out here with two scouts and a surveyor about a week ago. Nobody seems to know exactly what his graft is but he sure has got this post in a hell of a mess! I reckon Lieutenant Brannigan is still in command, though. He'll listen when I tell him I know who you are. He's bullheaded but he's square."

"Maybe you're forgetting something. You know who I am. So does Schwartz. The trouble is neither of you can be sure that maybe I'm not Brewster too . . . Who is this Brewster gent, anyway?"

Speers lolled back against the wall, carefully concealing the fact that he was talking to the prisoner. "Brewster is just about the top-hole outlaw in this miserable stretch of buffalo grass. He's been knockin' over stage coaches and killin' shotgun guards all along the lines. Been raisin' particular hell ever since the Injun fightin' died out. Orders are to shoot him on sight. I reckon you was plumb lucky Coulter and Yerg brung you to jail instead of lettin' Bonsall's plug-uglies shoot you."

Shelby frowned in surprise. "What's all that about the Indian troubles dying out?" he snapped. "It looks to me like they're just beginning. The Cheyennes are on the warpath and they're getting help from the Sioux, Kiowas and Arapahos."

Jeff sniffed with elaborate scorn. "Jest some refugees havin' a last fling," he scoffed. "Most of the tribes knuckled under six weeks ago. General Sheridan put on a winter campaign that knocked the varmints pop-eyed. For a dam' Yankee that Sheridan gent can fight! The Injuns tried to stage a bunch of their usual fall raids, figurin' to hole up for the winter lookin' innocent and drawin' government beef rations. The general surprised 'em a heap. He went after 'em while the snow was on the ground and they wasn't lookin' for any kind of trouble. By the time the first thaw come there was a lot of mighty tame Injuns around. Custer wiped out one village down on the Washita and the rest of our outfits have been cleanin' up stragglers from the Picketwire to Texas."

"Any big fights around here?"

"Nope. Nothin' broke loose this far west. Any war parties out here would likely be survivors of the Red

64

River fights. Maybe they're tryin' to stir up the peacefuls in this part of the country."

"They did it!" Shelby said bitterly. "But that's not my worry just now. I've got to make somebody believe that I ain't a bandit named Brewster. I wonder who I'm going to find on my neck, this Brannigan of yours or the other gent you boys don't seem to cotton to?"

Speers hesitated. "I reckon Lieutenant Brannigan is still in command so he'll be the one to try you. He's been here with a half troop since last fall. A week ago we had this Bonsall jigger drop in on us but he ain't takin' over any command that I can see. He seems to have some other kind of business on his mind but mostly he just bothers the lieutenant. Superior rank but no responsibility. It makes a mess for the lieutenant as you can understand."

"Is this Bonsall a tall, lean gent?" Tom asked. "I saw a captain just as I rode into the post. He was talking to the two galoots who later got so almighty anxious to ventilate my back ribs."

"That's Bonsall, all right. Ugly old coot with a hatchet face and a walrus mustache. He brung them other polecats with him when he arrived, them and that miserable calf of a surveyor. One of them must have been the cuss what called you Brewster."

Shelby nodded. "Sounds like Hogan. I don't suppose he remembers me — especially with these whiskers — but I know him from a fuss they had last summer back in Sheridan. He laughed himself right out of a mess with that chummy grin of his even though everybody knew he'd done murder. If he's at the bottom of this I wouldn't be surprised if the whole thing's a scheme to get rid of me and steal my peltries. He was looking at them mighty sharp when I rode in. It wouldn't take him long to hatch some kind of a smart plan to steal 'em."

"Pelts worth much?" Speers asked.

"Hard to tell. Might run close to a thousand if the market's good."

"That's bad! There's men on the frontier what'd hang their grandmothers for that much green. Hogan and Ike Pew fit right into that class. Better let me slip you a gun."

"Not just yet, thanks. I don't want to let myself in for a real outlaw charge. I'll stick around and wait my chance to clear myself."

"Suit yerself," Jeff grunted — "but I'll have a gun handy if things get to lookin' bad."

There was a moment of flat silence, then Shelby asked, "What kind of woman is this Mrs. Elson? She looked mighty stern at me a while ago. I'd hate to have her take a notion that she wants my scalp. Do you reckon she's the kind would get nasty notions about taking revenge for her husband?"

Jeff's lean shoulders hunched up in a lazy shrug. "She might — but it ain't likely. I never figured she was real keen on Gilly Elson. They arrived out here just before the winter set in and most of the boys got an idea that she's not all she makes out. She always treated Elson more like he was her coachman than her husband. Not that it made any difference to the fellers what tried to make somethin' of it; she just smiled at 'em and ignored 'em."

Shelby grinned. "Meaning you tried your hand?"

"Nope. Never had no time for wimmen. She's a right handsome gal, though. If a man had to have any truck with a female he couldn't hope to do much better."

Shelby's smile broadened. "That sounds mighty romantic for you, Jeff. You wouldn't be interested in putting in a good word for me, would you? Sort of keep her mind off her troubles and convince her that she hasn't any call to promote any necktie party for me. If she's got so much of a hold on all you boys I don't want her getting bloodthirsty ideas about the wrong man."

Jeff's sidelong glance was quizzical. "I'll see what I can do, Reb," he agreed — "but I'm still goin' to have that gun where I can reach it in a hurry. I'm a better hand at helpin' a man with a gun than I am at courtin' widdas."

CHAPTER
EIGHT

Steps on the parade ground interrupted the talk and Shelby moved back to the bunk. The more he thought about it the more it seemed likely that his guess had been right. Hogan had called him Brewster because it seemed like an easy way to steal the valuable furs. Whether the man knew him or not was doubtful. The whiskers had probably concealed his true identity but that would not have made any difference to Ed Hogan.

An hour passed before there was another chance for conversation. Then Jeff called in at the window, "You awake, Reb?"

"Sure. Why?"

"Somethin' up over at the tradin' post. Cap Bonsall jest went in there with Lieutenant Brannigan and them two ornery scouts. Maybe they're tryin' to get the gal's evidence on yo'. Better hope she gives you a good name."

"She can't tell much, I'm afraid. I never saw her 'til yesterday."

"Yo' didn't miss much, I reckon," Speers grunted. "What I saw of her didn't look like no art gallery. Is she as downright ugly as she looks at long range?"

"Hard to tell," Shelby evaded. "Most of her face is so battered and scratched that a man can't tell what she does look like."

The conference at the trading post seemed to be taking quite some time and Shelby paced his cell anxiously. It might be that his fate was being settled there. As the trooper had hinted earlier there was some sort of dispute in authority between the two army officers, a situation which might bring about almost any kind of break.

Presently Speers was relieved from his guard duty but he stayed to chat with the new sentry, obviously killing time. It wasn't long after that until there was a bustle at the door of the trading post and Shelby came to his window in time to see four men come out. The two in uniform headed directly toward the guardhouse, preceded by an orderly who had gone to meet them with a lantern.

In the flickering light Shelby could see that one of the men was the hatchet-faced Bonsall while the other was a younger man, a heavy-set officer whose sandy hair shone in the lamplight.

The sentry snapped to attention outside, Speers having disappeared discreetly. A nasal voice ordered, "Open the door, sentry. You will enter ahead of us, your carbine at the ready."

Shelby rose to his feet, standing with feet wide apart and his thumbs hooked in his belt. "Take it easy, soldier," he advised, noting the man's stern look. "I ain't making any breaks."

"Mind your orders!" Bonsall snapped. "Stand there by the door. The prisoner is a dangerous outlaw."

"On whose say-so?" Shelby demanded.

The officer's beady black eyes glared at him and Tom recalled the look he had once seen in the eyes of a dying Kiowa. There was something of a fanatic in this man, something which was doubly dangerous for its lack of reason.

Bonsall ignored the question and stepped closer to Shelby. He wasn't a coward, whatever his other faults or however timid he had sounded in his caution to the sentry.

"We want your story of the Indian raid," he said abruptly. "That unfortunate child at the trading post says the Cheyennes are killing and burning in the hills."

Shelby forced himself to be respectful. "They are, sir. I saw their war dance the other night and they're crazy for a fight. They had already killed Neilson when I watched them. His wife was brought in a prisoner then and she died shortly after."

Lieutenant Brannigan spoke for the first time. "The girl didn't tell us that, Captain. I understood that her mother was still alive. If the woman is dead I hardly think we are justified in ordering out a rescue party."

Shelby realized that the lieutenant was holding himself in check. Bonsall was his superior officer but Brannigan was not letting him have his own way without protest. Tom guessed that it was as Speers had hinted; Brannigan had the responsibility of the post but he was harried by a man who outranked him.

70

Bonsall's voice was coldly vicious as he faced the younger officer. "I think we should order out a strong force at once — in reprisal if nothing else. The girl says her mother is alive. We cannot dodge our duty to the woman just because an outlaw chooses to lie about it."

Tom restrained himself with an effort, a glance from Brannigan helping a little. Bonsall swung toward him again. "Where is this Indian village?" he demanded. "How many men are there?"

Something in his eyes betrayed more than a desire for the mere facts. Bonsall was excited about it.

Tom eyed him curiously. "Why ask me all these things? You don't believe what I tell you."

"Enough of that insolence!" Bonsall stormed. "You'll answer me, by God, or . . ."

Tom caught Brannigan's frown of warning. The burly lieutenant was not liking this interview any more than the prisoner. Probably because he was no more impressed with Captain Bonsall.

Tom spoke quietly. "You'll find the village near the head of Moccasin Valley, perhaps fifteen miles above the point where the White Water meets the Moccasin. There must have been sixty-odd Cheyennes in camp along with a sprinkling of Arapahos, Kiowas and Sioux. Maybe a hundred warriors altogether. However, there's no use trying to save —"

"I'll ask for your advice when I want it!" Bonsall snapped. He turned abruptly and headed for the door, speaking to Lieutenant Brannigan as he moved. "Lieutenant, you're in command here but I trust that you will honor my request for a detail. Supply me with as many men as you can spare. You must remain here at your post but the savages should be taught a lesson . . . after which I shall return to deal with this outlaw."

"Look here!" Shelby snapped. "I'm no outlaw! You had me thrown in here and you didn't give me any chance to say a word for myself. Here! I can prove who I am." He pulled an oiled silk packet from inside his shirt and displayed a number of papers, among them an honorable discharge from the United States Army.

Bonsall halted and turned to glance at the documents. Then he laughed gratingly. "Confederate deserter, eh?" he sneered. "I suppose you expect us to put a lot of trust in you just because you were once a dirty traitor and then betrayed your fellow criminals! You ought to be hanged on general principles!"

He flung the papers at Tom's feet and swung toward the door. The trapper started after him but Brannigan stepped hastily in front of him. "Easy," he warned, a trace of sympathy in his glance. "That won't help."

He stood firm until Tom got his anger under control, then he swung on his heel and followed Bonsall through the door. The sentry seemed to take a hint from the lieutenant. He lowered his carbine, a quirk of a grin making his ragged mustache waggle. "Keep yer shirt on, son," he advised in a low tone. "You ain't hung yet." Then he followed the officers out into the darkness.

For all his rage at Bonsall's boorishness Tom realized that there was still hope. He didn't know just what kind of a mess he was in but certainly Brannigan and his men had no time for Captain Bonsall. Just now they were in no position to help him very much but the hanging was at least postponed.

He went back to the bunk and sat down, trying to see the situation as a whole. First it had been the Indians who appeared as the real obstacle to his plans, now it was this lying banditry charge. He couldn't figure Bonsall's place in it. Bonsall was a thoroughly hateful character, a fanatic who might swindle and lie or even persecute those he hated, but Tom couldn't see him as a deliberate murderer who would kill a trapper for his furs. There is a personality in knavery as in everything else and Bonsall wasn't that kind of a knave. Still he was working with Hogan and Pew. Those two were capable of almost anything.

His mind switched to the Neilson angle. What had happened at the trading post? He felt certain that the Schwartzes would take good care of the girl but he couldn't understand what had happened to make Bonsall so ambitious. Maybe he wasn't a crude killer but just as certainly he wasn't the man to risk his hide in the rescue of an unknown immigrant woman — even assuming that he didn't believe Tom's story of Mrs. Neilson's death. That part didn't make sense any more than the rest of the tangle.

Shelby listened for the sound of Jeff Speers' return. Maybe the angular trooper was out digging up some information. Certainly it would be welcome. This business of sitting in jail, waiting in ignorance, was no fun.

CHAPTER
NINE

Across the parade ground a light flickered into being and Shelby could see that Bonsall and Brannigan were together in a building opposite the barracks. That would be Officers' Row — if the shacks deserved the term. He watched curiously, visualizing the scene which must be taking place. Periodically a shadow crossed the lighted window as someone paced the floor. That would be Bonsall, probably working himself up to some kind of a queer pitch. The man seemed to be a strange mixture of fanatic and adventurer. Brannigan would have a difficult time holding out against him if he was really set on leading a force against the village of Bear Nose.

The puzzling part to Shelby was this thirst for action on the part of a man who was obviously not an active officer. Bonsall had a commission but Tom would have bet money that it was simply one of those political appointments which had weakened both armies during the Civil War. The man didn't even have a command. Why should he now be so insistent upon a useless and hazardous expedition?

Suddenly Jeff Speers was back in front of the window, talking to the sentry — loudly enough to make

74

sure Tom would hear him. "Looks like the old boy is snortin' fer blood. Wonder what's got into him?"

"It don't make sense," the other man grumbled. "I reckon the man's jest nacherly crazy."

"Partly right," Shelby cut in — "but he's got some kind of an axe to grind. The crazy ones are the hardest to get along with if they happen to have big ideas."

The sentry muttered uneasily. "No conversation with the prisoner," he said, a bit uncertainly.

"All right," Tom agreed. "We'll both talk to Speers. He's dumb enough not to know the rules. Jeff, will you convey my thanks to your chum there? Tell him I appreciate his efforts. A while ago he made a good show of threatening me with his carbine — at Bonsall's orders. Bonsall never noticed that the gun wasn't cocked."

The sentry chuckled dryly. "Hell! I wouldn't mind any of his orders if I could get out of it. Anyway I'd jest as soon hit you over the head with the gun as shoot you."

"Bad judgment," Jeff remarked. "He's got a mighty hard head. If it comes to a fight your best bet is to shoot Bonsall."

The sentry's laugh was broken by the sudden sound of action from across the parade ground. The door of Brannigan's quarters opened to throw a yellow rectangle across the muddy ground. One man carrying a lantern moved down the line of houses while another ran across toward the barracks.

"School's out!" Jeff growled. "There's Bonsall headin' fer his quarters while the orderly goes to rout

out the men. Sam, it's lucky you and me is on guard detail. We'll be about the only ones left on the post."

They could trace the hurried preparations for the expedition even though there were no trumpet calls. Brannigan was superintending the job and he knew well enough that his men were within easy reach of vocal orders. It wasn't until Bonsall had routed out his gang that the activities of the post took on an air of noise and excitement. The strident triplets of "Boots and Saddles" rang on the night air, even though the men were at that moment in the stables saddling their mounts. Bonsall was obviously determined to make a military show even if he had to do it the ridiculous way.

Speers faded away into the darkness and presently a call came for the sentry. It left Tom alone and unguarded to watch the departure of the little column. He could see Bonsall and his two henchmen riding at the head of the troops, the fourth man of the mysterious clique not being in evidence. There were shouts from the corporal's guard left on duty and then the little body of troopers was swallowed up in the darkness.

Suddenly Tom realized that he had not slept in nearly thirty hours. The excitement had kept him from realizing it but now he knew that his eyes were smarting and his head was getting mighty weary. Even the thought that he was in jail in an almost undefended post didn't prevent him from falling asleep almost as soon as he hit the bunk.

It was broad daylight when he awoke. Some sort of scuffle was taking place just outside the window but before Shelby could move toward it he knew that another prisoner was being brought in. The door rattled and opened, two troopers appearing with a little man in civilian clothes. Judging by their cut he was an easterner. Judging by their appearance he had slept in them.

"Friend for ye," one of the troopers grinned. "The lieutenant said maybe you'd like company."

The little man stared at Shelby fearfully. "You can't put me in here with him!" he yelped. "It ain't legal! Suppose he murders me like he did those other people?"

"Good!" the trooper said solemnly. "If he does that we'll have some sure enough evidence on him. Right now the case has got a plumb bad smell."

They dumped the man on the floor and went out, locking the door behind them. Shelby stared in surprise. This fellow must be the surveyor Jeff had mentioned. Why had they thrown him in here?

There was no guard outside so maybe this was Brannigan's way of putting Shelby next to a source of information.

It would be a pleasure to work on one of Bonsall's gang but Shelby decided that maybe the easy approach would be the more effective one. He smiled cheerfully at the cowering man. "Buck up, friend," he advised. "I'm harmless. Captain Bonsall just made a mistake about me. Make yourself and your headache at home. We'll both have to sit tight 'til our luck turns."

The man eyed him with dull suspicion. He was battling a terrific hangover, that was clear, and he seemed to be having trouble in collecting his wits. "But Hogan said he remembered you well. You must be Brewster!"

So it was Hogan! Shelby kept his voice calm. "It's a natural mistake," he said. "Hogan didn't know me very well and I didn't have this beard then. I just seemed partly familiar to him and he got mixed up. It'll all come out in the wash. My name's Shelby. What's yours?"

"George Dombrek."

"How come they tossed you in the pokey?"

Dombrek looked bewildered. He was a bony little man with thin, sandy hair. Normally his eyes would have been a mild blue but now they were red-rimmed and bloodshot, a look of fright and perplexity in them telling Shelby that the man was ripe for a little judicious pumping.

"I don't know why they arrested me," Dombrek groaned. "Last night I got pretty drunk, I guess. When I woke up this morning I was on the floor in the room where I stay with Hogan and Pew. They were gone and so was Captain Bonsall. When I started out to look for them I fell off of my doorstep. That was when the lieutenant ordered me arrested. Drunk and disorderly, he said. I'm sick!"

"You'll live," Shelby told him dryly. "Lie down a while. We've got lots of time and nothing to do unless the Indians decide to raid the post while Bonsall's away with all the troops."

Dombrek shivered. The room was not cold and Shelby recognized the reaction as being partly fear and partly nausea. "Are the Indians really causing trouble?" the little man managed to gasp.

He was almost pathetic but Tom poured it on. "Sure. I wouldn't want to be in your boots. If there's anything an Indian hates most it's to see white men measuring the land they claim is theirs. Surveyors mean settlers and settlers ruin the hunting. A surveyor's scalp is the height of every warrior's ambition."

Dombrek dragged himself to the bunk Shelby had just left. "We're only working out ten miles from the line," he groaned. "Won't that be safe?"

"Ten miles from what line? The stage route?"

"Railroad survey line. It's about the same thing."

Shelby smiled grimly. "Worst place you could be," he assured his victim. "Indians hate railroads almost as bad as they hate surveyors."

The door opened again to disclose the trooper who had brought Dombrek. This time he carried food and made no pretense of keeping any weapon handy. "Better eat," he advised. "You sounded like a sawmill at breakfast time so we let you sleep. You had a lady visitor just after that but she gave one listen and hurried away. Do you make that noise natural or did you practice it?"

"Who was here?" Shelby asked. "Miss Neilson?"

"If that's the name of the cute little trick with the bandaged face. She seemed all worried about you — 'til she heard you snore. How's your partner doin'?" He jerked a thumb at the prostrate surveyor.

"Not so good. Every time he shuts his eyes his head aches so bad he thinks he's bein' scalped. It's good practice for him. The real article won't be such a shock when the time comes."

By the time Shelby had finished eating, Dombrek had dropped off into an uneasy sleep. Tom stared at him thoughtfully, trying to decide what Bonsall's scheme must be. The reference to ten miles sounded like some sort of game connected with the railroad lands. It could scarcely have any connection with his own predicament or with Bonsall's sudden ambition to fight Indians.

The meal made him sleepy again, the reaction striking him after the strain of the past few days, and soon he was snoring an accompaniment to the befuddled surveyor.

This time it was late afternoon when he awakened to find Lieutenant Brannigan standing over him. Getting his first good look at the officer, Tom saw that he was in his middle twenties, a jovial looking Irishman whose frown seemed out of place on his face.

"How long do you expect to sleep?" he asked, a trace of humor breaking the frown.

"Nothing else to do, is there?" Shelby retorted.

"Plenty. I want you to cover an outpost for us tonight. Will you do it?"

Shelby regarded him curiously. "Ain't you afraid I'll slit a half dozen throats and ride away in the dark?"

"Not seriously. Come on over to my shack and we'll talk this thing over. I don't like the position I'm in."

Tom had forgotten Dombrek but now the little man broke in petulantly, his voice showing that he was sober once more. "Excuse me, lieutenant, but how does it

80

happen that you release a known bandit while I am kept here for no reason at all? I must protest."

Shelby grinned and realized that Brannigan was fighting to keep a straight face. The frowsy little fellow's air of dignity was completely comic.

"I shall be glad to release you, Mr. Dombrek," Brannigan said smoothly — "if I have your word that there will be no more drunkenness. This post is seriously undermanned and we can't spare troopers to police our uninvited civilian population."

"But I'll be glad to help."

Shelby chuckled. "Sure. He'd like to kill off a few Indians before they start working on him."

Brannigan maintained his gravity. "Very well. Report to Corporal Crane. He needs a good man."

Shelby followed the officer from the guardhouse, aware that Dombrek had waited only a moment before coming out and heading across toward the barracks. Presently Brannigan murmured quietly, "Crane is handling the mess sergeant's duties. I hope he'll make good use of our little friend."

Neither of them spoke further until they were in Brannigan's shack of an office. Then the lieutenant asked abruptly, "How much truth did you tell Captain Bonsall?"

"It was all true."

"You think that the Cheyennes are planning to attack this post?"

"There's a fair chance of it."

"What about the Neilson family? How well do you know them?"

"I never saw any of them until the night I saw Mrs. Neilson being brought in by the Cheyennes. The next morning I found the girl in the forest. The rest of the story I told you a while ago."

"But what about this mysterious packet which Mrs. Neilson is supposed to have carried with her when she was taken. I have an idea that Captain Bonsall is taking that part of the story quite seriously."

Shelby stared in astonishment. "I didn't know anything about it," he said slowly. "What kind of a package was it? Who says she had one?"

"Miss Neilson seemed much concerned about some sort of valuable package her mother was carrying. She was a bit vague as to its nature but she seemed highly impressed with its value. Are you certain that she didn't mention it to you at any time?"

"Not a word. Maybe she didn't trust me. She might have been willing to confide in army officers when she wouldn't talk too carelessly before a stranger."

Brannigan eyed him doubtfully but nodded. "That might be it. However, that's not what I brought you over here to talk about. I'm inclined to believe your story and I want to make you an offer . . . Your release in exchange for your services while we're short-handed."

"And when Captain Bonsall comes back?"

The lieutenant shrugged. "I cannot speak for Captain Bonsall. He is my superior officer, you know. I'll take the responsibility of releasing you now but I can't promise anything for the future."

"Meaning that if I see fit to ride away during the night it'll be my own risk?"

"I can't discuss that. I merely make you an offer. Call it a request if you like. I want an experienced man on the picket tonight, a man who knows Indian fighting. You will be joined by a trooper shortly before daylight so that we'll have double guards at the danger hour. I can't promise a thing after my contract with you is complete."

Shelby smiled ruefully. "It isn't much of an offer but I reckon I'd better take it. Where will I find my guns and ammunition?"

"At the barracks. I anticipated your agreement and I sent one of the men to draw equipment for you. A change of clothes isn't much to offer for the work but it's more than nothing."

The trooper in charge of the equipment-drawing detail proved to be Private Jefferson Speers, late of Mississippi, Alabama and points west. "They tell me you're turnin' honest for a couple of days," he greeted. "Here's yore stuff — although what you want of junk like fryin' pans is beyond me!"

Shelby laughed aloud. Speers had taken the officer at his word and had drawn a complete outfit, including all camp equipment. "You better take most of that stuff back or the government will have a real banditry charge against me," Shelby told him. "All I want is clothes."

Blue breeches, a flannel shirt and underwear made a welcome change and he was glad to discard his worn moccasins for a pair of stout cavalry boots. "That's all I want," he said when he picked up the articles. "I'll go bareheaded before I'll wear one o' them bummer's caps again."

His own six-gun and Spencer carbine had been placed with the other articles, a supply of ammunition provided for each. It took only a matter of seconds to clothe and arm himself, then he motioned to Jeff. "Come on, soldier. Better come tell the stable sergeant that I'm to have a horse. I've got to stand guard over you pilgrims tonight."

CHAPTER
TEN

It was a dreary chore, circling the post throughout the long night but it gave Shelby plenty of opportunity to think. He felt reasonably certain that he understood the general nature of the game Bonsall was playing but the other parts of the puzzle wouldn't fit. A scheme to grab government land wouldn't account for the false banditry charge.

He spent the hours of darkness trying to figure out some way to clear himself but nothing sensible would come to mind. Always he came back to the realization that the whole matter turned on Hogan's identification of him. He would have to fight it out with Hogan, that seemed a certainty.

Shortly before dawn a trooper rode out to join him, a low whistle announcing the man's approach. Lieutenant Brannigan had kept his promise to double the guard for the danger hour — or maybe he was just sending a picket, expecting that Shelby would have departed during the night.

Tom recognized Speers when his low hail came, "Hiyah, Reb. I see the outlaw is still stickin' around for the hangin'."

"Sure. No point in runnin' off like I was admitting anything."

Jeff halted beside him, a dull blur in the pre-dawn blackness. "Glad to find you, Reb," he said soberly. "It's best to stay and fight it out. Makin' tracks now wouldn't settle anything for you."

"That's what I figured. I was almost tempted to slope just to see what Hogan's scheme might be. It'd show up pronto if I escaped."

Speers laughed shortly. "And now you'll have to guess. Anyway, you kin always hope that the redskins will take care of him for you."

"I can't hope for that. There would be too many other fellows in the same jam out there. I wonder how the expedition is making out?"

"We'll soon know. They oughta be comin' in sometime this mornin' — if everything went good . . . I reckon it did or there'd ha' been some refugees stragglin' along by this time."

Shelby forced his mind back to the business at hand. "We better look to our own chore, Jeff. If there's going to be an attack it'll be coming soon. The coyotes have quit their singing. That means dawn. Swing off there to the south and I'll circle in the opposite direction. Careful when we meet each other on the opposite side. This is no time to be making any mistakes."

Within the hour it was clear that no attack was coming. Either the savages had no plans for attacking Fort Butler or the Bonsall expedition had caused them to keep their warriors in the hills. Leaving Speers to continue the day patrol, Shelby rode into the barracks, turned his mount over to the trooper on stable duty, and reported. Brannigan took his report without comment, seemingly content to ignore the doubtful status of his scout.

At the barracks the troopers, including the men who had arrested and guarded him, seemed anxious to show their good intentions. When he asked for barber tools he was quickly supplied, Trooper Jim Coulter doing yeoman service in the hair cutting department. Before many minutes had passed Shelby was able to see a strange face in the little mirror which hung near the barracks doorway.

"I don't look quite so much like a bandit, anyway," he observed. "I hope Bonsall will be impressed."

Corporal Crane winked broadly at a couple of grinning troopers. "The hell with Bonsall! You're thinkin' about that blonde gal at the trading post. Don't worry! She'll think you're right purty."

"Rats!" Tom retorted, vaguely irritated at the suggestion. He had been keeping similar thoughts from his own mind and it bothered him to find that others were thinking the things he had kept from himself.

"You might do a heap worse," Coulter chuckled. "Mebbe you ain't seen her since she shucked outa that bull hide sack she was wearin'. That gal's put together nice!"

"I know," Tom said shortly, recalling his first impression, before he had realized that she was not a squaw. He turned away deliberately and stretched out on an unoccupied bunk. He had intended to visit Schwartz immediately but now he decided to let the matter wait. No use letting these cheerful idiots think he was all steamed up about the girl.

He fussed around the barracks until after the noon meal, taking out his spite on Dombrek who was serving most unwillingly as a cook's helper. The little surveyor was cold sober now but he was still jittery. Tom tried to work on his fears in order to extract information but the fellow obviously knew little. He had been hired to survey the land along the proposed extension of the Kansas Pacific Railroad but he was not in the full confidence of his employer.

Shortly after noon Shelby strolled casually over to the trading post, hoping that he had allayed the barracks gossip. He wouldn't have admitted it to anyone but he was looking forward keenly to seeing Karen again. Maybe she was pretty; maybe she wasn't. One way or another she had been a mighty good partner during a bad time.

He rounded the corner of the store and came face to face with the woman he had seen at the door of the stage station. A single glance told him that he had been quite right in estimating her as a woman of marked charm. Today her eyes held none of the tension which he had noted in them before. Instead there was a hint of warmth there, a friendliness which still failed to break her quiet dignity. Jeff had called her a mystery woman; certainly she was not the type to be expected in such a place.

She seemed to be waiting for him to speak and he seized the opportunity.

"Mrs. Elson?" he asked.

88

"That's right." Her voice was throaty without being harsh, a voice that seemed to blend well with her air of self-possession.

"I'm Tom Shelby, the man they arrested the other day. I hope you'll believe me when I tell you that I'm not the bandit they claim I am."

She smiled slowly. "I believe you," she said simply. "Schwartz was just telling me about you. He seems pretty certain that you're all right."

"I'm glad somebody thinks so. Most of the time folks seem bound to make me a pariah."

"Not everybody," she corrected. "You had another friend relating your virtues last evening. Private Speers makes quite a character of you."

Tom grinned. "Private Speers is quite a character himself. I might add that he has some strongly complimentary ideas about you."

Her smile broke out in a flash of amusement. "That's enlightening. He never mentioned it to me."

"Jeff's bashful," Tom explained dryly, "but he's not blind."

She eyed him with frank interest. "That sounds suspiciously like a neat compliment. I'm flattered."

Something in her glance dared him to continue the small talk. He met the challenge. "Glad to oblige," he said easily. "Always happy to perform small services of that nature when I don't have to lie."

She flashed him a quizzical look as she picked up her skirts and started out into the rutted trail. Then her voice lowered subtly as she replied, "A generous offer, I'm sure. I'll look forward to the pleasure."

He couldn't make up his mind whether she was laughing at him or not. Somehow he didn't believe that she was. He watched her until she turned into the crumbling ruin which served as her home, then he grinned to himself and pushed open the door of the trading post.

Schwartz was industriously chewing the stub of a pencil as he pored over some accounts, trying to make believe that he had not been watching the meeting outside. He rose with an embarrassed grin as Tom entered.

"Hallo, Tommy," he greeted. "Der poys toldt me you proke der chail oudt."

"Sure. I bit a hunk outa the bars and slipped through while my stomach was empty. The place was too confining for my delicate health."

"Undt now you vant to see der young leddy, is dot it?"

"Not particularly. I came in to get a hat. Good broad-brimmed felt. Got anything better'n the usual line of moth-eaten stuff you sell to tenderfeet and Indians?"

Schwartz sputtered indignantly and began to sort over a pile of hats on a rear shelf. "Vot size?" he glowered. "Big enough to fit der head or der ideas?"

Tom smiled. "About a seven and an eighth, I think."

The rear door opened and the strident voice of Mrs. Schwartz interrupted the deal. "So yez wheedled yer way outa the calaboose, hey?"

Shelby lowered his voice dramatically. "Of course. I couldn't stay away from you another minute. Your old man was here when I came in so I'm stalling him off with some talk about buying a hat. We can't let him know about us, can we?"

"Don't git gay with me, ye young divil — jest because ye've got yer face scraped 'til ye look indacent! Ye're not so handsome, me gossoon. To my way o' thinkin' ye're better lookin' with the whiskers; they hid more o' yer ugly phiz."

"Thanks, Mom. You're kinda cute yourself now that I think of it."

"Of all the blatherin' young cubs! Git on in the house wid yez! I'll stay here with Schwartz and pick out a hat that'll hide plenty o' yer face."

Shelby chuckled and sidled past her toward the door. Karen must have been listening to the conversation for she stood near the doorway, smiling in a mixture of amusement and welcome. Her damaged eye was hidden under a bandage but Mrs. Schwartz's treatment had already done wonders for the rest of her face. The angry scratches had lost some of their fire and Tom realized that his first hunch had been right. This girl was really a mighty attractive young lady. Even when compared with a charming woman like Mrs. Elson she stacked up mighty well.

He took her outstretched hand, holding it just a little longer than was necessary as he inspected the cut of her trim gingham gown. He wanted to tell her what he had just discovered about her but instead he asked, "How's the eye?"

"Doing nicely, thank you," she murmured. "Mrs. Schwartz has been babying me a lot but I like it. It has been a long time since I've had anyone to pamper me like this and I'm taking dreadful advantage of the opportunity."

She seemed so cheerful that Tom hated to tell her of her mother but he knew the job had to be done. Already there had been enough confusion because of her ignorance on the subject.

"I came to tell you something which I should have told you before," he began slowly. Then as her quick look told him how wrongly she was guessing he hurried on. "I'm afraid you will have to give up any hope of ever seeing your mother again."

She stared in surprise but her reply was firm. "I'll never give up hope while there are still soldiers out looking for her. I feel sure she will be rescued."

It was hard to go on from there but Shelby plunged on. "I'm sorry," he said. "That's what I should have told you before but I couldn't make myself do it. Your mother died right before my eyes." Better to blurt it out like that than to fumble around and prolong the agony.

She dropped down heavily on a bench and Tom went on with the story, cursing himself silently for his awkwardness. He avoided her eye as he spoke, trying desperately to make her understand that her mother's death had been quick and painless.

She was silent for some moments after he finished the recital. Then she spoke, almost in a whisper. "Maybe it was all for the best. I should hate to think of her being a prisoner."

Tom dropped down on the bench beside her. "Forgive me for not telling you sooner," he said softly. "It was a hard thing to do."

She reached out to let her hand close over his long fingers, her grip telling of her effort at self-control. "You were very kind," she said simply. "I'm afraid that if I had known I could never have forced myself to the effort of making that journey in from the hills."

He nodded. "Maybe I was thinking of that when I kept quiet. I couldn't afford to have you let down while we were in such a tight place. We couldn't have made it if you hadn't been pulling your weight like a real trooper. You see, I was looking after my own interests."

She forced a wan smile. "Nonsense! Don't try to make yourself out as selfish. You . . ."

"Careful!" he warned. "You'll have me getting pleased with myself. Anyway, I want to be selfish again. I want you to help me out of the fix I'm in now. For some reason Captain Bonsall is after my scalp and I've got to figure out why he is so set on getting it. Lieutenant Brannigan is well disposed toward me, I think, but I've got to find out what Bonsall's game is if I'm going to protect myself."

"I'll do anything," she told him. "I'll swear that you have been with me for the past month. There's no one alive now who can prove anything different."

Her sincerity brought him a quick satisfaction. She was forgetting her own grief in her anxiety to help him. "Thanks," he said simply. "I don't think we'll need to make a perjurer of you. I have an idea that if I can get a line on Bonsall's graft I'll know something about how to tackle the problem. I understand that you told him something about a valuable packet which you believe your mother was carrying when she was taken prisoner. Did you give him any more information than that?"

She frowned a little. "I'm afraid I hinted more than I intended to but I believe Captain Bonsall left here with a wrong idea. It all happened when the two officers were getting ready to leave after they had talked with me. I felt that they were not intending to do anything about my mother so I referred to the bag again, speaking to Captain Bonsall alone and trying to impress him with the importance of a rescue attempt. It seemed to change his attitude."

"Just what did you tell him — if I may ask?"

"Let me tell you the whole story. I'm afraid I don't know how much of it I gave away in my anxiety to get help for my mother."

"You don't need to confide in me if you don't want to. All I'm interested in is getting a line on Bonsall."

"You had better know. As I told you before, my parents were rather well fixed financially. When we fled from Denmark my father decided to turn everything into some form of security which would be salable in any country, some form which would be easy of transportation. In Holland he bought diamonds. Some of the stones were sold to provide money for our living expenses before we came west but the rest of them were sewed into a little chamois bag. My mother always carried the bag under her skirts except when we were at home. Then she hid the bag in a hole in one corner of the dirt floor."

94

Tom's eyes had opened wide at the story. No wonder a leech like Bonsall had been so excited and anxious to hit the trail for Moccasin Valley. "Diamonds!" he exclaimed. "That's a new one on me. Most of the excitement in this part of the world has been over gold. Do you think your mother really had the bag with her when she was captured?"

"I feel sure she did. Of course I couldn't see what happened in the cabin while the Indians were attacking but I believe I know what she would have done under the circumstances."

Tom nodded. "At the first sign of trouble she would have taken the packet from its hiding place and secreted it on her person."

"Exactly. Unless . . ."

"Unless what?"

"Father was wounded, remember. Maybe in the excitement of the sudden attack and in the haste to help Father she might have been too busy to make the transfer."

Shelby rubbed his chin thoughtfully, the newly shaven flesh strange to his touch. "Then the bag may be in any one of several places. It may still be in the ashes of your cabin — or under them. In that case there will be an excellent chance of finding it. If your mother carried it away with her we must figure on a lot of possibilities. I don't believe the Indians would have searched her so it's a fair bet that she still had it when she reached Moccasin Valley. If it was still on her person when she died I'm afraid you will have little chance of recovering it. Certainly some Indian would have found it in the ruins when they disposed of her body."

He noted the girl's quick horror at the reference and he plunged on quickly, trying to divert her with a question. "Do you believe that she would have buried the bag in the tepee if she had been given the opportunity?"

Karen nodded, trying to steady her voice for a reply. It hurt to think of her mother's last moments but she steeled herself for the effort. "I believe she would have buried it at the first opportunity. Mother was quite a hand at hiding things. That's why she took charge of the diamonds in the first place."

"Good. I feel sure that she had her chance. I watched that lodge for fully twenty minutes as I worked around toward it — and one of the points I was most interested in was whether or not she was alone. I don't believe there was anyone in there with her at any time."

The girl's glance came up to meet his. "Then you were trying to . . . ?"

"Never mind that. I didn't make it . . . How much of this story did you tell Bonsall?"

"Only a part. I felt that I had to make every possible effort to get help. I told them my mother was carrying a valuable packet. It didn't seem to make much difference to the lieutenant but Captain Bonsall held back and asked me if the bag was really very valuable. I told him it was and he seemed satisfied. The only thing he asked after that was whether my father was raising crops or cattle. I told him neither and he went out."

"But you didn't mention diamonds?"

"No."

Tom smiled grimly. "I'll bet I know what he thinks. Any crooked land hog in his position is always thinking of gold. He figures your father was a prospector and the bag is full of samples or perhaps the map to a mine strike. Every time there's anything mysterious in this country everyone smells gold."

"Do you think he would rob me?"

"You bet! No matter what he thinks he's looking for he'll take whatever he finds."

"But I need them," she said simply. "Father made an arrangement last autumn to have cattle driven here this year. A friend of his who wanted the diamonds was to finance the purchase and take the diamonds in payment. I must have them to meet my obligation when the cattle arrive!"

CHAPTER
ELEVEN

The full meaning of her words silenced him for a few moments. He remembered her grim determination in the valley, her spoken promises to return there. Evidently she hadn't just been talking. She really felt it her duty to go back there and carry out the program her father had planned. At a time when there was enough sorrow in her mind to overshadow all else she was still thinking in terms of the task she had to perform. Somehow it made Shelby a little impatient with himself. If Karen Neilson could go forward there was no reason for him to be fussing about his own difficulties.

He patted her shoulder awkwardly. It would have been satisfying to do more but he didn't want her to think that he was taking advantage of such a moment. "We'll hope for the best," he said, trying to sound optimistic. "Maybe Bonsall won't get things figured out right and will hunt in the wrong place."

"But suppose the diamonds are gone completely? Maybe no one will ever find them."

He looked down at her, conscious that she was altogether appealing in spite of the bandaged face. The trim curves of her body brought back a quick memory of that first meeting when he had treated her so roughly. "If you're stuck I'll make a deal with you," he offered, forcing back the thoughts which had come into his mind. "I was figuring on locating in the Moccasin but since I talked to Bonsall's surveyor I'm afraid my site would be within the ten mile belt of railroad grants. I don't want to get settled on railroad land so I reckon I'll have to move back into the White Water. I'll have capital enough to stock up with some pretty good Texas cows — after I get my peltries sold. Maybe we can work out some sort of a partnership deal."

"What kind of a partnership?"

He fumbled before her steady glance. "Any kind you say. If things work out all right and they don't decide to hang me we'll be dividing the White Water range between us. Maybe it would be a good idea for us to pool our efforts until we can get a good start. It will be easier than trying to work separately."

"But what do I have to offer in such a partnership? You're the one who will be supplying all the capital — and most of the work."

He grinned more confidently now. "I'll risk being abused. You're the same kind of a lone wolf I am. We've got the same kind of ideas, looks like, so I reckon we'll get along. There's lots of ways we can trade off chores."

Her tone was a serious copy of his own. "I'll need a good strong ranch hand and you'll need a cook. If we don't locate too far apart I can do the cooking and the lighter chores while you act as range boss for both outfits. Doesn't that sound big when you use such words?"

He smiled his satisfaction at the way her spirits were coming back. She seemed to have an amazing ability to take her bumps and come up smiling. "We'll make it big," he told her — "if the luck will only make a bit of a turn. I warn you, though, that I'm a real Jonah."

"I'll take the chance," she said. "If you'll promise not to let those miserable whiskers grow again I'll risk having you around for a while."

"Who's taking the chance?" he demanded with a fine show of belligerency. "You've seen my face but I've never seen yours. How do I know how homely you're going to be when you get all your hide back on?"

"Have it your own way," she retorted. "So it's your risk . . . although I can't see what my face has to do with a ranch deal."

"Don't worry about it. I won't. I knew you were a winner before I ever had a look at your face — in any condition."

She frowned in perplexity at the statement, then blushed prettily as she remembered. "You certainly were thorough," she murmured. "Scared as I was I think I still must have blushed."

He took her hand again. "If you did it didn't show through all that dirt and leaf mould you had on your face."

"Don't make me think of it. I must be pink now. Shall we shake hands on the deal?"

He slipped an arm around her shoulders. "Couldn't we do better than that?"

She made no move to draw away but how far her agreement might have gone he didn't learn. At that

100

moment the door opened and Mrs. Schwartz stuck her head in. "Sorry to bother yez, kids," she said with a knowing wink — "but the guard out there was jest bawlin' somethin' about a column of sojers bein' in sight. I reckon Tommy better climb down off'n his pink cloud and git ready to do battle with that ugly Bonsall spalpeen. Ain't it too bad the ould divil had to pick this particular instant to come back?"

She ducked out of sight as quickly as she had come, leaving Tom and Karen to make what they could of the moment. Shelby jerked his head toward the closed door. "There's a lady," he said. "I don't care how she talks; she's a lady!"

"And a mighty kind one. Now what are you going to do about your problem?" She had slipped away from him as Mrs. Schwartz interrupted and was now standing, her color still high but her eyes full of concern.

"I don't know yet," he said, very much let down. "I'll have to see how things work out."

"I'll be watching," she promised. "If it begins to look bad I'm coming over to tell them a story that will either clear you or have me in a jam of my own!"

He smiled again, amused but grateful. "Don't be hasty. If there's anything you can do I'll let you know. You can always trust Jeff Speers if you're in doubt about anything and I am unable to get word to you. Don't worry about it. Things are bound to come out right now; I've got a partnership business that has to have my attention."

★   ★   ★

From the porch of the trading post Tom could see that the plain toward Moccasin Valley was clear of riders. For a moment he was puzzled, then he saw that a sentry was staring out across the parade ground toward the east. That was odd! Why should Bonsall have returned in such a roundabout way as that?

He hurried around the building and crossed to where he could get a clear view. Lieutenant Brannigan hailed him at once, smiling as though a load had been lifted from his mind. "Looks like good news for both of us, Shelby," he said. "That's quite a sizeable force coming in from Fort Wallace. It settles my problem for me and it will probably help you at the same time. Somebody with this column will surely outrank Captain Bonsall."

"I hope you're right," Tom replied. "Judging by the baggage train they must be coming out for a real campaign."

Brannigan smiled. "You didn't look very close — or you've forgotten your army days. They've got everything in that wagon train, including company laundresses. I'd guess that the orders have come through to turn Fort Butler into a major post. Probably a headquarters while the railroad work is going on."

They watched in silence as the bluecoats filed into the open quadrangle. Two companies of the Tenth Cavalry and a detachment of mounted colored infantry with a considerable baggage train. Brannigan's guess seemed good.

"That's Major O'Rourke in command," the lieutenant remarked, leaving the doorway to walk toward the newly arrived officers. "He's a square enough man for anybody. You'll get justice now."

Tom watched idly while the troopers dismounted and busied themselves with the work of settling into their new quarters. The negro troops were taking over some of the buildings beyond the main barracks and Shelby grinned at the sight, wondering how Jeff was reacting. During the war there hadn't been anything quite so infuriating to a Confederate as the sight of negroes in uniform. What would Jeff say to this?

Somehow it didn't occur to him that his own detached thought in the matter was unusual. These men were good soldiers; their workmanlike manner showed it and it didn't cross his mind that he would once have resented their presence. A lot of his old prejudices had left him within the past few years. A few more had gone within the past few minutes. Maybe the world wasn't such a bad place after all.

In such cheerful mood he returned promptly to the trading post and found everyone out watching the new arrivals. Karen was talking pleasantly with Mrs. Elson, the two of them making a pleasantly contrasted picture.

"It looks like the Indian scare is all over now," he observed. "Enough men in the post now to fight a fair-sized war."

Karen was not diverted by the comment. "What will it mean to you, Tom?" she asked abruptly. "Will this help you to prove your innocence?"

"I hope so," he replied. "Brannigan thinks I'll get a fair shake from this new commander."

Mrs. Elson looked surprised. "Surely they're not continuing to claim you're Brewster, are they?" she exclaimed.

Tom shrugged. "I reckon Bonsall and Hogan are still set on it. That's why I'm plenty glad to see somebody in charge who is more likely to give me a trial instead of going on with the hanging."

"That's ridiculous!" she said angrily. "When so many people know you I can't see how Captain Bonsall would make such a mistake."

Once more he had that uneasy feeling that maybe she was laughing at him. Then he caught the full power of the brown eyes and he knew she wasn't. She had moved over to stand close beside him, the friendliness in her smile bringing him a strange conflict of emotions. It was pleasant to sense the admiration of such an attractive woman but it was also a little disconcerting. Karen had fallen silent and Tom knew without looking that she didn't like the way Nan Elson was behaving.

"It'll all work out," he said vaguely, conscious that he ought to make some remark to break the tension. "Maybe I won't have to fight the case at all. Bonsall has been out so long now that it's a fair chance the Indians will have answered the prosecution with their hatchets."

Karen turned away suddenly and Tom couldn't tell whether it was because of the reference to Indian killings or whether the girl was simply annoyed at his sudden attention to Nan Elson.

Suddenly he knew that he didn't understand either of these women very well. Karen seemed so fragile and

104

tender, making a man want to protect her. Still she was a sturdy campaigner when the occasion demanded. There had been nothing fragile about her when she shot the Oglala. She had been the independent one when they were hiding in the glade. She was certainly displaying no weak tenderness in her plan to go back to the White Water.

Mrs. Elson was another kind of a paradox — but a mighty interesting one. She talked lightly as though carrying on a planned but meaningless dialogue. She never sounded quite serious but her eyes betrayed her. She wanted the attentions she had missed out here on the frontier. It might be dangerous to banter too much with Nan Elson. She was very much a woman behind her pose of humorous unconcern, a woman whose ideas might take almost any turn.

Mrs. Schwartz filled the awkward gap in the conversation. She was standing where she could see the front of Officers' Row. Turning to Shelby with a crooked smile she jerked a bony thumb toward the parade ground. "Here comes a trooper, Tommy. I'll bet it's yer ownself he'll be lookin' for."

It was Coulter, the lanky trooper who had once arrested Shelby — and helped him outwit Bonsall's scouts. He pulled down a corner of his mouth as he faced the little group, apparently not quite certain of the nature of his errand. "Lieutenant Brannigan wants to see you, Shelby," he announced. "There's somethin' brewin' over at his diggin's. Old Ramrod O'Rourke is pacin' the floor like he's got a good old-fashioned mad on about somethin' or other. Hope you ain't in his black book like you was in Bonsall's."

"Me?" Tom grimaced. "Why should I be in anybody's black book? I'm everybody's friend. If anybody wants a goat for anything all they need to do is hunt Shelby. They are tickled pink to have me around for that purpose. What's this O'Rourke gent mad about?"

Coulter shrugged uncomfortably. "I ain't in the major's confidence. Maybe it won't be bad."

"Well, let's go." Tom's voice was grim. "There's a chance he wants me to come get a medal — but I'll sell my chances cheap. I've got a healthy superstition about officers in bad humor. They're plumb bad luck for me. Better get the guardhouse swept out."

He turned to the others. "So long, folks. You can come visit me later."

Nan Elson smiled encouragingly. "We'll be hoping for the best. Maybe you'll come see us instead."

Karen didn't say anything.

CHAPTER
TWELVE

The sentry at Lieutenant Brannigan's door seemed to have none of Coulter's misgivings. He grinned cheerfully at Shelby and passed him in without announcement. Brannigan and Major O'Rourke had evidently been in some sort of heated discussion but there was no evidence of ill feeling between them. The big, red-faced major was obviously impatient about something. Brannigan was grim but a light of satisfaction showed in his eyes. Tom suddenly knew that he was not coming in for anything very troublesome.

O'Rourke acknowledged the brief introduction and snapped crisply, "Let's have the whole story, Shelby, omitting nothing even though you have already reported it before. We may have to move quickly and I want to know all I can."

"What story?" Tom asked. "About the Indians or the bandit business?"

"The Indians, of course. The town marshal at Sheridan hung that Brewster outlaw last week. Forget about that and tell me what sort of a mess Bonsall has run his fool head into!"

Tom caught Brannigan's quick grin and suppressed his own sigh of relief. This was his lucky day. First Karen and now this!

He repeated his story just as he had told it to Bonsall. When he had finished, O'Rourke pointed to the rough map on Brannigan's wall. "Where is this Indian village?" he asked abruptly.

Tom pointed out the approximate location.

"Has Captain Bonsall had ample time to make the raid and return?"

"Plenty, sir. Even allowing for unusual delays he should have been back early this morning."

O'Rourke stopped his pacing. "Then we'll go after him! Lieutenant, how many men do you have fit for duty?"

"Six, sir. Captain Bonsall requisitioned almost the entire command. Shelby has been serving as a volunteer."

O'Rourke swung abruptly, his gray eyes boring into Tom's. "You are now employed as a government scout," he snapped. "Regular terms. Take it?"

Tom grinned a little at the manner in which the offer had been made but he replied readily enough, "Yes, sir. Now could I make a suggestion?"

The officer's brusqueness relaxed a trifle. "That's what you're hired for. What is it?"

"Don't order the men out just yet if you're figuring on a relief party."

"Why not? No reason for delay, is there?"

"Several, sir. The men must be tired and they would make very little progress before dark. If you let them

108

rest until midnight they'll be fresher and the easy end of the trip will come during the hours of darkness. It will be daylight before we reach rough country and we'll make better progress. We'll get there just as soon and the men and horses will be in better shape."

O'Rourke didn't hesitate. "That's the order, Lieutenant," he told Brannigan. "Will you see that it is passed to the company commanders? Have the men get as much rest as possible between now and midnight. Captains Bent and Gorse will take thirty men each and be ready to move at twelve o'clock. Two days' rations and a hundred rounds of ammunition. Lieutenant Burke will follow at dawn with ten wagons and a half company as guard. You will continue in command here until I return."

Tom set about his preparations with grim dispatch. This O'Rourke talked like a fighter. He knew what he wanted but he had the sense to accept advice from men who knew the situation. It was going to be a pleasure to serve under such a commander.

A cavalry mount was assigned to Shelby and for the next hour he was busy. A load had been lifted from his mind but there was no point in ignoring his new danger. He was going into combat. This expedition wasn't going to be any picnic and a smart man would take plenty of care with his preparations.

It was nearly dark when he felt satisfied that everything was ready. Then he headed toward Schwartz's store. Before reaching the building he stopped in at the trading post stable to look at his horses. Useless whinnied softly at his master's approach and Tom saw that the big roan had been rubbed down until his coat glistened. Obviously Dutchy was taking mighty good care of the animals.

"Hello, boy," he said gruffly. "Sorry you can't go with me this trip. Government job, government hoss takes the chance of stopping Indian lead. You behave yourself and maybe I'll be back to give you some more mean treatment."

The roan seemed to understand, as usual. He bumped his nose against his master's shoulder, waiting to have his ears scratched. Shelby obliged — briefly — then turned away and left the stable without another word. The worst part of this job would be leaving Useless behind but he was glad to take the cavalry horse. He had no desire to risk the big roan in a battle.

He went in through the back door of the Schwartz domicile, knocking sharply before pushing the door open. Karen and Mrs. Schwartz were working in the kitchen.

"In time for supper?" he asked solemnly.

Mrs. Schwartz scowled amiably but her intended retort was blocked by Karen's swift question. "Is everything all right?"

He bowed with exaggerated dignity. "The authorities at Sheridan hanged a bandit named Brewster last week. Your humble servant, Thomas Benton Shelby, is now an honest citizen in the employ of the United States Army."

Karen's astonishment made her falter. "You mean — you have enlisted? Then you won't be . . . ?"

"The partnership is still on," he said firmly. "I made a temporary contract to help a shanty Irisher named O'Rourke drive the Indians out of *our* valley. Nobody but a dumb bog-hopper would pay a man to clear his own land."

Mrs. Schwartz rose to the bait. "Shanty Irish, is it?" she shrilled. "Bog-trotter, hey? I'll have yez to know, me bucko, that it's the Irish what are makin' this country safe for the likes of yez!"

Tom laughed delightedly. "Easy, Mom," he cautioned. "You'll have these other assorted immigrants jealous. With a Dutchy and a Swede in the house you'll have to mind your manners. Squareheads are mean when they get aroused."

"Manners, is it! And when did ye git the right to talk about manners? Callin' honest folks squareheads and the like! What do yez think yez are?"

"Sort of a mongrel," he replied cheerfully. "What difference does it make — and what are we having for supper?"

Karen seemed to be getting considerable amusement out of the byplay but her mood seemed definitely reserved as the meal progressed. She asked questions about the proposed expedition but Tom could sense that she was holding herself in check. There was none of the warmth in her manner which she had shown earlier in the afternoon. Either she had changed her mind about him or she was still resentful of the interest he had shown in Nan Elson.

He found no opportunity to thresh the matter out but when he was leaving he asked abruptly, "Is anything wrong? You've been so quiet I'm almost afraid you're repenting your decision on that partnership deal."

"Not at all," she assured him. "It is still a very generous offer on your part. I just hope it will work out all right."

She offered her hand and he took it, disturbed that this should be the way of it. Then he was out in the darkness, making his way across the parade ground to the barracks. Maybe it was just as well the parting hadn't been emotional. A man never knew what might happen on a trip like this.

At eleven-thirty the fort was astir. Horses were saddled to the accompaniment of good-natured grumbling but otherwise there was little being said. Sleepy men, faced with another long ride, this time into hostile country, had no urge for idle chatter, and this time was no different than usual.

A hearty meal was eaten, despite the hour, and at twelve sharp the column headed out toward the hills; Major O'Rourke, Captain Bent of B Company and Shelby taking the lead. Tom chuckled silently to himself as he rode along, vaguely amused that he should so readily have slipped back into military service. Many times he had sworn that he was done with soldiering for a country which offered him nothing but abuse — but here he was, not exactly a soldier but certainly on a soldier's errand.

Strangely enough there was comfort in the thought. The darkness behind him was filled with the familiar sounds of cavalry on the march. Hoofbeats in the dirt.

The creak of leather. Jingling accoutrements. The occasional laugh as comments passed along the line. It was all part of the life he had known, a life which hadn't been so bad for all the circumstances which had brought him into it. Back there in the darkness were men he didn't know but who would be ready to give him help if he needed it. After so many months of playing a lone hand it was a mighty comforting thought.

His only regret was the memory of the way he had left Karen. After a brief glimpse of happiness it was too bad to have the bubble burst so soon. Perhaps when he returned he would be able to move forward again. The Indians would be out of the valley and . . . He laughed shortly. That was certainly getting well ahead of things!

The column halted once, watering the horses at the crossing of a clear creek which they reached just as the first streaks of gray were diluting the eastern gloom. No stop was made for breakfast; any man feeling hungry so soon after a big meal could draw on his iron rations.

At daylight the pace was speeded even though the trail was getting rocky as they entered the foothills. Already they had passed the junction of the White Water and the Moccasin and were pushing on rapidly when a lathered pony came around a bend, its rider low in the saddle.

Shelby could see the advance guard hailing him but the man did not stop until he reached Major O'Rourke. It was the trumpeter from Brannigan's troop, his eyes bloodshot but his face stretched into a smile as he surveyed the blue column behind O'Rourke. He pulled his horse up sharply, snapping a brisk salute. "Message from Captain Bonsall, sir," he announced, as though he had been fully aware that he would meet help at this point. "The command was attacked by a large force of Indians just before daybreak. I got through just before they closed in on this side. The captain requested a diversion to draw them off but I guess you will want to do something different from that."

O'Rourke nodded grimly. "We will! . . . But I can't imagine what kind of a diversion Bonsall expected Brannigan to make with six men."

Shelby put in a question. "What Indians attacked you? The ones you struck when you first came out . . . or didn't you make the attack?"

"We cleaned out one village day before yesterday. Then we went into camp. The outfit that jumped us this mornin' was mostly Sioux."

The messenger had swung in beside the officers, obeying O'Rourke's motioned order. The major looked up sharply at this last bit of information. "How did it happen that you were still in the valley if your attack on the village took place two days ago?"

"I don't know, sir. It was Captain Bonsall's order. We went into camp on this side of the Indian village just after we wiped them out. Orders were that the men should rest while a detail went into the village to destroy it."

"That surely didn't take two days, did it?" O'Rourke snapped.

114

"It seemed to, sir. Captain Bonsall took the two civilian scouts with him. No enlisted men were detailed to the work."

O'Rourke stared but asked no further questions. If the trooper had any idea of what this strange conduct meant he didn't seem inclined to mention it. O'Rourke couldn't very well ask for mere gossip about another officer.

Tom could have told him but he wasn't talking either. Bonsall had learned enough from Shelby's account of Mrs. Neilson's death to guess that there was a fair chance of the unfortunate woman having buried her valuables. He must have been poking around in the village in an effort to find some trace of burial. No other reason would seem to account for his doing all that work while enlisted men lay idle so near at hand.

O'Rourke broke in with another question. "How far ahead is the fighting?"

"Half an hour of hard riding, sir. Maybe less if our men have been able to fight their way down the valley."

"How many Indians are in the attacking force?"

"Couple hundred, maybe. They made it plenty hot, sir."

O'Rourke grunted. "We'll try to return the compliment. This may be our chance to break up the last gasp of the Indian resistance."

The men were pressing forward with enthusiasm but Major O'Rourke deliberately slowed the pace. A difference of minutes wouldn't be so important at this stage of the fight and he wasn't going to send his men in on exhausted horses. It was slightly over the estimated half hour when the sound of firing could be heard from up the valley.

"They're holding out!" O'Rourke exclaimed with satisfaction. "We're in time. Shelby, what's the lay of the land?"

"Mostly flat on this side of the stream, sir. The ground rises steep on the other bank."

"Fair enough. We'll drive a wedge into the savages on this side and make a junction with Bonsall . . . Orderly! My compliments to Lieutenant Gordon. He is to take thirty men and deploy to the left while the rest of the column continues along the creek. Maybe he can strike the savages in the rear after we turn them away from Bonsall."

Almost before the rear guard detached itself for this duty, the flitting forms of Indians could be seen among the pines ahead. The fight had settled down into some sort of siege, the main battle continuing just a short distance beyond.

Bugles blew the charge — unnecessarily, for the blue column had dashed forward at sight of the warriors. Shelby rode beside O'Rourke in the lead, his mind curiously enough being chiefly occupied with anger at the government's economy program. Many of the Indians ahead were armed with the new Spencers or Henrys while the troops charging behind him carried the old single-shot Sharps. The Sharps was a fine carbine but it was outdated, a fact which the government elected to ignore. Many of them were on hand as left-overs from the Civil War — so they had to be used regardless of need. It was a fortunate thing that

116

the Indians had never become as proficient with the rifle as their ancestors had been with the bow. Traders might supply them with modern weapons but no trader could make an excited warrior pull his front sight down!

Even as the thoughts raced through his mind, Tom drove his pony directly into a little knot of warriors. They were Sioux and the idea of defensive fighting on foot was not appealing to them. All along the line the Indians were breaking before the charge, waiting only for a hurried shot or two before seeking cover. Using his six-gun while the troopers around him slashed out with sabers, Shelby broke through the Indian lines and whirled to come back. The triumphant yells of Bonsall's men indicated that they were dashing in to close quarters and a heavy burst of firing from the flank told of Lieutenant Gordon's thrust.

Attacked thus from all sides the Indians broke in panic, only small groups huddling together for last desperate stands. The whirling, slashing mass of struggling figures made any sort of planned fight impossible and Tom ceased his charging tactics. There was no point in trying to cover the whole field: it would be enough to kill only the enemies who directly threatened him. After all, this part of the job was for the troopers.

He pulled up deliberately and rammed fresh charges into the Navy Colt he carried. It was becoming difficult to distinguish friend from foe in the smoke but the sounds of fighting told the story. Bonsall's right flank and the flankers under Gordon had turned the savages back into the trap sprung by O'Rourke's main force. The Indians were in the nutcrackers and were being exterminated.

Tom ranged his pony toward the center of the fight, almost immediately spotting the grinning face of Hogan in Bonsall's line of jubilant troops. Hogan met his gaze at the same instant and Tom caught a flash of something like fear in the man's fading smile. Even in the fury of the battle he realized that Hogan knew him, knew him as the trapper who was supposed to be in the Fort Butler guardhouse, the trapper who had been cold decked for a fancy fur robbery.

Suddenly, two mounted Sioux broke out of the smoke cloud and drove straight at Tom, one of them levering a cartridge into his Henry carbine while the other reached out with a lance. Tom whirled to meet them, aware that Hogan was raising his gun.

The cavalry horse reared up as the Sioux thundered in and there was a swift flurry of desperate action. Tom and the Indian rifleman fired almost in each other's faces, Shelby swerving as he fired, avoiding the lance of the second warrior. The move threw him off balance and in the same split second he felt his horse stagger under him.

He realized that he was being pitched headlong over the pony's head — directly toward the bloody knife of a third Indian who had come running up behind the others.

Even as he fell he knew that his horse had been shot in the side of the neck as he reared up — a shot which

118

must have come from the side where Hogan was standing . . . a shot aimed at the rider!

There was just time for the thought, then he was hurtling down upon the running Indian. He struck blindly with the barrel of his gun but a swift stab of pain knifed at his ribs and something seemed to wrench sickeningly at his shoulder. Then the sound of battle died away and the world went black.

CHAPTER
THIRTEEN

Shelby's return to consciousness was a gradual matter of feeling more and more pain. The entire upper half of his body seemed to be one big ache and it was some time before his mind could shake off the fog of nausea. Then he realized that the scene about him was familiar, as though he had been aware of it during the period of unconsciousness.

Stars shone brilliantly overhead although there was still the suspicion of a glow in the western sky. Fires gleamed among the trees at a little distance and for just an instant Shelby felt a shiver of alarm. Suppose they were Indian fires?

He knew immediately that the fear was unfounded. The Indians had taken no prisoners in that fight: any savages who had gotten themselves away had been lucky. Around him he could hear the strained murmurs of wounded men and he twisted his head a little in an effort to see. It brought a stab of pain to his left side and shoulder but it brought something else, the attention of a strange voice at his side.

"Made up your mind to live, did you?" a mild voice asked. "How do you feel?"

"Awful! I think a horse stepped on my head and skated down my left side. What happened to me?"

"I don't know. I was a little too busy about that time to be watching anyone else. All I know is that I got a bullet through the leg. The sawbones patched it up and set me here with orders to let him know when you stopped breathing."

"Don't go away. I might quit any time. Breathing is a lot of trouble just now."

The other man laughed. "You ain't hurt. Anybody that talks about what happened to him is too curious to be in bad shape — even if you have been out cold for hours."

"How did the fight go?"

The man laughed again, a note of bitterness in his voice. "The official report will announce that a large party of hostile Sioux and Cheyennes was completely exterminated by our gallant troopers — at slight loss to our side. That will be partly right. We killed a lot more of them than they did of us but the fact won't be any help to those men wrapped in blankets out there. It might make my leg hurt less but fancy words can't cure a slashed throat."

Tom smiled a little at the philosophy as well as at the precise accents of the speaker. This fellow's story would probably be as strange as his own. He didn't sound like the sort to be found in the border service.

"How many men did we lose?"

"About a dozen, I suppose, not counting some of our chums around us here who won't recover. It was a real fight for about fifteen minutes. Then the Indians broke for the hills and we chased them until the major called us back. It was right at the last that I had to be fool enough to get my leg in front of Indian lead."

"Did the major get hurt?"

"I don't think so, although he was right in the thick of it all the time. It looked as though every Indian in the fight was trying to count a coup on him but he seemed to come through without damage."

Tom wanted to ask about Bonsall — and about Hogan — but the effort had already used up his scant supply of energy. It was easier to lie back and wait for the next step. He was still alive and in good hands. The rest could take care of itself.

He dropped off into a dull slumber which let him forget his aches, sleeping by snatches through a long night that seemed to be full of disturbing sounds. At daybreak he was awakened by two troopers who were trying to lift him as carefully as possible. They tried to save him as much pain as they could but every touch was agony. He was placed in one of the rough wagons which were being used as ambulances, and the long trip back to Fort Butler began.

Throughout the day he was jolted around with other wounded men, sometimes partly unconscious but generally wracked by the pain in his ribs, shoulder and head. Once they halted while he was fully awake and a surgeon came to look after his patients, changing a dressing here and there and generally doing what he could for the men.

"You'll soon be as good as new," he told Tom cheerfully. "You took a nasty crack on the skull and I was afraid you wouldn't regain consciousness. Now that you're awake, though, I guess you'll pull through."

"Good thick head," Tom smiled wanly. "What's the reason for all the rest of the aches I seem to have?"

The surgeon grinned. "You've got all the symptoms of a kid who took a dive into a dry millpond. Your left shoulder is bruised — and probably sprained. There's a knob on your head the size of an egg. All of that looks like some kind of a fall. The only honest battle scar you're going to have is the knife slash across your ribs. Sorry, but no bullet holes to show your grandchildren."

After that the jolting horror of the trip was like some prolonged bad dream. Once Shelby woke to full consciousness, realizing that he had been delirious. There was a confused memory of Major O'Rourke talking to him but he couldn't quite separate the recollection from his visions of Hogan trying to kill him in the battle.

Eventually the ordeal came to an end and Tom knew that he was being carried to a cot in the barracks. One end of the long building had been curtained off as a hospital, the post not supporting any such extravagance as a real medical establishment. It was night again when the wagons were unloaded and Tom scarcely cared what was happening to him. It was enough to find himself on a cot which did not bump or roll. Soon he slept, not the semi-consciousness of shock but real sleep.

When he awoke it was broad daylight and the room was bright with warm May sunshine. Speers was working over a trooper two cots away but presently the gaunt southerner turned to find Tom watching him.

"Hello, Reb," Jeff grinned. "Finally made up yore mind to wake up, did yo'? I never seen sech a feller fer sleep!"

Tom moved as though to rise but sank back quickly as pain slashed through his left side. Jeff clucked warningly. "Lay still, yo' loon! Yo'll open up that gash. How'll I keep my new job as hospital orderly if my customers don't behave theirselves? Be quiet now and take it easy."

"What's the news?" Tom wanted to know.

"Yo' fellers are about all the news there is," Jeff grinned. "But I hear there's considerable of a stink over in Officers' Row. Major O'Rourke's plenty hot over the way Bonsall left his men in a trap. Bonsall won't talk."

"What's the story? I'm pretty much mixed up on what I saw, what I heard and what I've been dreaming."

Jeff lowered his voice and came closer. "All I know is the gossip — and some of it don't make sense. After our boys cleaned out the Cheyenne camp they set right smack dab down on their tails and waited while Bonsall and his two pizen pups put on some kind of a diggin' bee. Judgin' by what Captain Bent's men found, Bonsall musta spent the whole day diggin' around where the Injun tepees had been burnt down. Got any idea why?"

"Won't Bonsall tell?"

"Seems not. He just claims he was tryin' to recover somethin' valuable fer your tow-headed gal friend. By the way, she's runnin' around with her whole face

124

showin' now and it's worth a second look. You better dang site git up outa that cot as soon as yo' can or half the command will be tryin' to cut yo' out. Business has been mighty good for Schwartz lately, what with all the boys fakin' errands at the tradin' post."

Tom grinned, his question almost inaudible. "I wonder if Bonsall found anything?"

Jeff stared at him curiously. "None of the boys know what it's all about but they'll give odds that he didn't get whatever it was he was after. Him and his pards was still diggin' when night caught 'em and the next mornin' they was too busy combin' Injuns outa their hair for them to go on with their chore."

"Didn't they hunt any more after the fight was over?"

Jeff laughed aloud. "They sure didn't! From what I hear there wasn't none of 'em dared look cross-eyed after Major O'Rourke got done cussin' 'em out. Anyway, the whole valley got afire toward the end of the battle. That put a crimp in everything. It was a fire that mighta meant ruin for the whole foothill country except that a heavy rain came along just before dark. That stopped the fire before it ever got out of Moccasin Valley."

"I must have slept through all that," Tom muttered. "I don't remember any rain."

"You slept through a lot," Jeff agreed. "That blonde gal was in here most of the night. She and Nan Elson did the work of two danged good surgeons. If ever I get any holes blasted in my hide I just hope I get such good attention. They was a bloody lookin' pair by the time mornin' come but they stuck it out. More'n one lad in here owes his life to 'em!"

A pale trooper on a nearby cot grinned weakly. "That's right — and I'll pay my debt any time at all. Either one of 'em can have me for the askin'."

"Generous, ain't you!" Speers gibed. "Offerin' sech a valuable carcass to a couple o' pore homely females what can't find a man to take 'em!"

He turned to face Tom quizzically. "I reckon I'll have to get busy with that widda woman, Reb. She was givin' you so much of her time last night that she had the blonde gal actin' plumb worried. If they hadn't been so busy I reckon we mighta had another battle right in here."

The volley of acid comment which came from the surrounding cots brought a quick order from the surgeon. Jeff moved away to attend his duties as hospital orderly and Tom was left to ponder over the things he had heard.

The remarks about Karen and Nan Elson he could take with a pinch of salt. It didn't surprise him that they had taken over emergency duties but the rest of it was probably a figment of Jeff Speers's humorous imagination. He didn't doubt that there might be a coolness between the two women; Karen's attitude had indicated that such might be the case. However, he felt certain that there could have been no such tension as Jeff had hinted.

The other parts of the story were satisfactory enough. The Indian threat seemed definitely over and the Neilson diamonds were not yet hopelessly lost.

126

Captain Bonsall had not found them, even though he had been shrewd enough to figure on their being buried in the Indian camp. Maybe the packet had been destroyed by the same bolt of lightning which killed Mrs. Neilson. Or could lightning destroy diamonds? Tom didn't know and the detail bothered him as he tried to figure out the situation.

Lieutenant Brannigan entered the room and came straight to Shelby's side. "Feeling better — Brewster?" He grinned, something in the quirk of his smile warning that this was not merely a social call.

"I'll be up tomorrow," Tom assured him. "I just got clumsy at the wrong time."

"Not so fast," Brannigan protested. "Doc says you'll be a star boarder for a long week, at least."

He sat down close enough to the wounded man so that he could talk without being overheard.

"Have you heard from Miss Neilson this morning?"

"No." Tom was rueful. "I just woke up."

"I understand. Major O'Rourke and I went to see her just after breakfast. She still insists on being very secretive about the nature of that packet her mother is supposed to have carried but she told us a little more about the matter. It seemed clear to Captain Bonsall that there was something to her story so Major O'Rourke is just curious enough to want to take a hand. He feels that Bonsall is trying to frame something off color so I'm heading out at daylight, taking Miss Neilson and a full troop. My orders are to make any efforts Miss Neilson may direct in an attempt to recover her property. The major is curious but he is also bound that Captain Bonsall won't cheat a girl who has appealed to the army for help."

"That's mighty decent of you," Tom told him. "Do you think it's safe to take her along?"

"Don't be jealous! I'm tickled to death to have such company but I didn't have any say in the matter. She simply announced that she would go. I suspect that she would make the trip if she had to go alone."

"She would! . . . Lieutenant, will you try to arrange it so that your search of the cabin ruins is handled with a bit of tact? No use putting her to the pain of seeing the remains of her father there in the ashes."

Brannigan nodded soberly. "The burial detail will go ahead — with strict orders. Meanwhile, let me give you a word of warning. So long as I have gone out of my way to be unethical and talk about a fellow officer — though I hate to use the term for him — I might as well drop all pretense of trusting the man. Six new plug-uglies came into town this morning to join Bonsall's surveying crew. I don't know how soon he's going out on that job but you'd better look out for yourself while he's around the fort. He blames you for all the trouble he got himself into — and a couple of those scouts of his don't exactly admire you."

"So I gathered," Tom said dryly. "One of the polecats tried to shoot me in the battle. It was his shot that dumped me into the lap of an Indian. I'll be ready for 'em if they give me a chance to get out of this pill shop."

"Take it easy. I'm posting picked guards for this detail, men I can trust with a little knowledge. I'm

128

about fed up with brevet captains raising hell with my post! . . . You'll be all right while you're in here but watch out for yourself when you get on your feet!"

"Where are the men staying? There certainly can't be much room left in the barracks."

Brannigan gave him an odd look. "They've holed up at the stage station. Mrs. Elson has extra room there and she seemed glad to have some boarders."

He seemed to expect some reaction to this news but Shelby made no comment. He was trying to decide whether this new tie-up would have any significance.

CHAPTER
FOURTEEN

Shelby was dozing in the pleasant warmth of midday when he heard Doctor Bacon's cheery voice raised in a word of good-humored greeting. The surgeon seemed to be on joking terms with everybody in the command but Tom realized that this was not quite the salutation he would have given one of the men. His voice held that indefinite note of half caress which creeps in when an older man tries to be jovial with a pretty girl — a kind of resentful fatherliness.

"Hello there, nurse," Bacon was saying. "Are you coming to cheer me up or to make fever cases of my star boarders?"

"You're an old flatterer, Doctor," came the retort in the softly clipped accents of Karen Neilson. "You'll make me vain talking like that about me."

"Do you good to spoil you a bit," Doctor Bacon retorted with a laugh. "Fine test of character."

She had halted just inside the doorway, the rays of sunshine dancing in the nimbus of bright hair. Only a faint red mark remained under one eye to recall her recent injuries and that one spot could do little to spoil the fullness of her charm. Jeff had been stating it mildly when he said she was worth a second look.

The oval of her face was perfect but the twinkling blue eyes and slightly tilted nose gave her an air that was more than mere cold beauty. Her fair complexion and pale hair might have qualified her as one of those legendary northern princesses but the pert nose and merry eyes changed the picture to something infinitely more human. There was beauty enough in Karen Neilson but there was also a warmth and life which made Tom wonder at his own blindness. This couldn't be the forlorn girl he had pitied so benevolently just a few days ago!

She caught the full meaning of his gaze and came toward him, blushing a little as she answered the greetings of other men in the room. Many of them she had nursed the night before but they seemed to know that this time her errand was no business of theirs.

She stopped beside Shelby, taking his hand in hers. "I heard you were better," she said simply. "You had me pretty worried last night."

"And now you've got me worried," he retorted solemnly. "I can see where I'm going to have plenty of trouble. A man can't expect any peace of mind when he goes into business with a partner like you. Half of the time I'll be neglecting my chores to look at you and the other half I'll be busy chasing other men away."

She laughed politely but her voice held a note of strain as she asked, "And how will you find time for the — er — entertaining you do so well?"

He started to protest but she silenced him with a gesture. "Don't bother to answer that. I didn't come in to talk nonsense. There are several things I want to tell you about before Doctor Bacon chases me out. I'm going back to White Water Valley tomorrow morning and I want your advice — and some other help — before I go. Major O'Rourke has been very kind about everything and he's sending a detail out with me to help me get settled."

"Settled!" Tom echoed in astonishment. "I understood that you were simply going out with a patrol and would come back with them. You can't risk going out there alone!"

The red lips tightened just a trifle. "My place is out there," she said firmly. "The scouts report that there are no Indians left in the region. In that case I have no excuse for idling around here. There is work to be done in the valley and I must get at it as soon as possible."

Again she cut short his protest. "No arguments, please. The surgeon will invite me to leave if I get you all stirred up. You know what our plans are. I'll be all right until you come out to join the firm — if you are still thinking of going through with it."

He almost swore. What a time and place to make such remarks! He wanted to tell her how wrong her suspicions were but he restrained himself. Instead he reached for her hand again, his voice low. "I've been several different kinds of a fool in my time, lady, but I was never an idiot — and there's nothing wrong with my eyes. Now that I've seen you with all your hide on you couldn't drive me away!"

"I thought we had dropped the nonsense," she reproved. "We can't run a partnership on gallant speeches — even though they do seem to come easy to

you. I need equipment and I need money. Mrs. Schwartz has offered to stake me but I thought you would prefer to avoid outside capital."

He smiled at the way she put it, embarrassed at having to ask him for money even as she uttered her veiled reproach. "I don't like the idea of you being out there alone — but you can draw on Schwartz for anything you need. I've been building up a balance with him for three winters now, not counting this last one. Get what you need and don't skimp. We'll still have enough left to cover the cattle deal."

His eyes warned her to say nothing about the way she had planned to pay for the herd. It was just as well to keep the fragment of the secret safe.

He tried to prop himself up on an elbow and the effort cost him a nasty twinge in the wounded side. At his grunt of pain Doctor Bacon came over quickly. "Too much excitement," he scolded. "You need absolute quiet until the shock of this thing is over. Otherwise you won't be able to do anything about business for weeks. Lie quietly and don't move that arm."

"I'll go," Karen said meekly — "since that remark is evidently a diplomatic hint for me to do so. I suppose it's just as well. If I have to do all the work for the company I can't afford to idle around here."

"Let him alone," Bacon laughed. "Unless he's crazy he'll waste no time in getting on this job! Talk about combining business with pleasure!"

Tom released her hand reluctantly. He would have given a lot to be able to talk to her alone for a few minutes but this was no place for him to say what he wanted to say. He would have to take what consolation he could from the fact that she still intended to be a partner. "Take care of yourself," he said seriously. "Be sure to carry the Henry and take plenty of ammunition. I wish you'd ride Useless. He'll be safer for you and he must be needing the exercise. I'll use the pinto."

She gave him a long look before she replied. "Thanks, partner," she said finally. "I'll take him. He has gotten to know me pretty well since I've been caring for him."

"Oho! So you're the one who has been getting him all shined up! We'll elect you wrangler for the company."

"I'll drop in before I leave," she said, backing toward the door. "You must rest now."

Even after she was gone it was difficult for Tom to get himself settled down. Evidently she had been having doubts of his sincerity but he didn't let that worry him. She still had her sense of humor and he felt confident that once away from Fort Butler he could convince her. What a partnership this was going to be!

He found himself almost fearful of the thought. It was too much to expect. The past few years had been hard ones and the past weeks had been especially full of troubles. A man couldn't hope to have his luck change so suddenly.

Starting with such an idea it wasn't difficult for his thoughts to trace the line of troubles which seemed to be in the offing. Perhaps the Indian threat was over — but what of Bonsall's crowd? Even though he was still only guessing at Bonsall's purposes it seemed clear that the Moccasin and White Water valleys would never be entirely peaceful while the ex-Carpetbagger and his toughs were roaming the hills. Certainly it was no country for a girl to live in alone.

Speers came in for a few minutes in the evening, reporting much activity around the trading post. Tom had been fretting at the thought of Karen doing so much of the work that he should have done but Jeff laughed when it was mentioned.

"Don't yo' worry about that gal workin' too hard," he chuckled. "I never seen so many lazy sojers in my life what suddenly got ambition. All the gal has to do is look around and right away she's got a half dozen o' the boys fightin' to see who can run errands for her."

"Maybe that's what bothers me," Tom said. "I suppose yo've been shining up to her just like all the others?"

"Who — me? Shucks! I jest went around to see that the boys didn't git uppity nor nothin'. I was goin' to curry the hosses fer her but there wasn't none to do but the pinto. Some o' the other boys was already scrubbin' down the pack nags and she wouldn't let nobody but herself touch that big roan. She treats that crowbait just like he was human."

He lowered his voice to a confidential whisper that could be heard across the room. "Jest between yo' and me, Reb, I got a notion it ain't you she wants — it's the hoss. I wouldn't blame her."

"I wouldn't either," Shelby agreed. "Useless has got more sense than most men I know — including a lanky —"

"Funny name fer a hoss," Speers interrupted. "Yo' warn't by any chance doin' honor to a certain Yankee general when yo' picked out that name, was you, Reb?"

Tom grinned. Jeff was simply trying to kid him into good spirits but the effort was worth a reward. Adopting the same stage whisper he replied, "As one Galvanized Yankee to another — yes. Don't let it get around."

Somehow the banter made him feel better and presently he dropped off into a sound sleep.

He was awake at reveille and it wasn't many minutes before he heard voices in the gray dawn outside. Karen and Lieutenant Brannigan came in together, the girl flushed with excitement over her preparations but still carrying her air of brisk efficiency. She had discarded the gingham dress for a new pair of buckskin breeches and the blonde hair was pretty well concealed by a broad-brimmed hat. Still she made a picture which quickened the wounded man's pulses.

"Last-minute council of war," she greeted cheerily. "We need some questions answered."

Tom didn't like the way she was including Brannigan in that "we" but he managed to conceal his feeling. "What kind of questions?" he asked. "About the equipment?"

She perched lightly on the edge of his cot, taking his hand. "We won't even talk about equipment," she laughed. "I'll leave you that shock until you're well enough to stand it. When Schwartz tells you how much I bought you'll probably want to dissolve partnership."

Her voice dropped to a whisper as she leaned tantalizingly close. "What we want is a description of the spot where my mother was killed. We're going up Moccasin Valley to see if there is any likely place that the other searchers missed. After that we'll cross the ridge into White Water Valley and search there."

"I still don't like the idea," he said aloud. "The Indians are likely to come back. You've had enough troubles without going around looking for more."

Brannigan cut in quietly. "I think the Indian danger is definitely past, Shelby. We have had patrols out constantly and there has been no sign of any hostiles since the fight. I think the whole trouble was pretty much of an accident that won't be repeated. Refugees from the southern fighting found their way up here after General Sheridan's winter campaign. They were pretty mad, of course, and they happened to meet up with some Sioux scouting parties who had ranged down from Wyoming. The Sioux have been pretty cocky since Red Cloud closed the Bozeman. They probably worked on the Kiowas' anger and stirred up the whole mess, the local Cheyennes being caught in the current. It's all over now."

Tom rolled his head gingerly in doubt. "Indian danger is never over. Suppose the Sioux come back with help?"

"It's scarcely likely. There's nothing here to attract them. Now stop worrying and tell us what we want to know."

137

He came over within easy whisper range and Tom grinned a little as the three of them put their heads together so soberly. "Conspirators!" he hissed dramatically, feeling a little better at the levity. "Well, there isn't much I can tell you. It was dark and the storm was coming over as I watched. All I remember was a level camp site where Moccasin Creek ran along the sheer face of the north canyon wall. It's just like that for several miles so I don't suppose the description helps. However, you might look for a spot which shows signs of having been burned."

"We won't have to look for that," Brannigan reminded him. "The whole valley burned after the battle. We'll try everything, though. I'm not only anxious to help Miss Neilson recover her property: I'd like to get it right out from under the nose of a certain party we all know too well."

"Keep a good watch every minute," Shelby warned him. "It's a dead certainty in my mind that the gang is working a two-way graft — not counting the sandy they tried to run on me. If Bonsall has added some new plug-uglies to his string it's a cinch he's expecting his game to pay dividends."

Brannigan frowned.

"Want to tell me what you think the game is?"

"No reason why not. I figure it's the old land grab in the first place. Bonsall is using his army connections to front for some land outfit. When the Kansas Pacific goes through they'll get title to alternate ten-mile strips of land. If the land is valuable it will be thrown open to purchase. If settlers are already on it they will be allowed to buy at minimum rates. Bonsall's survey gives him a first look at the land so he can gobble up the spots which are likely to become big centers."

"But how does that get him into this business of interfering with Miss Neilson?"

Shelby smiled thinly. "Ever hear of a bandit who would stick to one robbery when an easier and bigger one was thrown under his nose? The same men who were hired to act as settlers and hold the land can be used to hunt for what Bonsall believes is more valuable. He probably figures he's on the trail of mineral wealth. Naturally he'll try to use his organization to grab that instead of some bit of doubtful railroad property."

His jaw set a little more grimly. "Of course, Bonsall would have no objection if a couple of his boys picked up a bit of side money by robbing a trapper of his pelts."

Brannigan nodded. "It sounds reasonable. We'll keep an eye on the gentlemen."

He stood up suddenly. "I'll go get ready," he said aloud. "Three minutes to say your farewells, young lady. Don't spoil this big waddy: he's too confounded lucky now!"

"No need for delay," she said hastily, rising from the edge of the cot. "We've settled everything, I guess."

She avoided Tom's eyes. "So long, partner," she said, trying to sound casual. "Doctor Bacon promises you'll be around in ten days. Don't be foolish and delay your recovery. I'll be needing help with the work."

Then she turned and hurried toward the door. Tom expected to hear a rush of banter when she was gone but to his surprise none of the men said a word. Suddenly he knew the reason why. They were thinking of Karen and Brannigan teamed up. No matter what the circumstances it was a hazardous proposition to let a pretty girl start out into the hills under the protection of a personable man like the lieutenant. The men had noted the change in her attitude toward Shelby and they had decided it was no longer a joking matter. Tom knew they were right and swore softly into the rolled blanket which served him as a pillow.

CHAPTER
FIFTEEN

The ride up Moccasin Valley was pleasant enough. Spring was in full course now, the green shoots struggling bravely with the dead grasses along the creek banks. Karen rode silently beside her pack animals most of the day, trying vainly to take a hand in their supervision. The men would not permit it, however, and she was left to enjoy the sense of security which came to her. Almost for the first time since leaving the old country she knew what it meant to have active assistance and the prospect of a good future.

Brannigan rode ahead of the column. Only twice had he dropped back to speak with the girl, once at the crossing of the White Water fork and the other time when the command halted for lunch. Both times he asked a perfunctory question as to how Karen was standing the long ride. He was courteous but certainly not attentive.

In late afternoon they came upon the scarred area where the battle had been fought. Brannigan halted beside the circle of shallow rifle pits which Bonsall's men had dug, motioning for a lanky sergeant to ride forward. Karen followed the man and heard Brannigan's terse question.

"How were the men disposed here, Andrews?"

"Our boys were right here, sir," the sergeant replied, pointing to the trenches. "We dug these holes under fire, using our spade bay'nits and mess kits. The Sioux hit us first from the other side — up the valley. Then they circled and caught us from all sides. Some of 'em had gone up the ridge there and were beginning to fire down on us when Major O'Rourke arrived. He came up over the same trail we did, strikin' the Injuns in the rear. After that most of the heavy scrap was back there in that brush we just rode past."

Karen looked back curiously. That must be where Tom had been injured. She tried to imagine the wild scene which had filled the now peaceful valley but her thoughts were interrupted as Brannigan asked another question.

"Where was the first fight? Your attack on the Cheyenne village?"

"Just through that clump of firs, sir." Andrews pointed ahead.

"And the valley is all burned beyond that?"

"Yes, sir."

"Then we'll make camp here for the night. Select the camp site and take charge. Miss Neilson and I will ride on a short distance and look things over. I suppose it won't be necessary to detail men to take care of her pack horses?"

Sergeant Andrews grinned. "No, sir. I'll have to detail somebody to let 'em alone and do the rest of the work."

142

Brannigan smiled and led the way toward the fir thicket which Andrews had indicated. Karen followed, neither of them speaking until they were threading a passage through the trees. Then Brannigan explained, "We can't do much here today. Might as well avoid the burned area for camping purposes and figure to make our search in the morning."

She nodded silently, wondering at the subtle change in him. Somehow he had dropped the brusqueness of the day and was more as she had seen him at Fort Butler. She had been curious about his silence during the day but now he puzzled her more than ever.

In a few moments they broke out into an opening which was a perfect picture of desolation. At the right Moccasin Creek babbled along in the shadows under the cliff but the rest of the valley seemed to be one vast scar. Directly before them the ground had been torn up as though angry mastodons had battled over a circular half acre. Every bit of turf had been turned over, leaving the soil to be washed out in little gullies by the rains. Beyond this bare spot was the burned area, singed brown trees rising like scarecrows here and there out of the forbidding black earth.

It was a depressing sight but Brannigan laughed. "I wouldn't have believed it if I hadn't seen it with my own eyes," he murmured.

Karen stared at him curiously. "What?" she asked.

"All this hand plowing. Imagine three men doing all that work for nothing! Three such men as did it, too."

The girl's answering smile was checked as she suddenly realized the significance of this torn area. "I wonder where it was that my mother died?" she said slowly.

"I'm sorry," Brannigan apologized. "I had forgotten."

"No matter. I have no right to throw my troubles on you. It's over now."

He pointed across the village site and lifted his reins. "Let's look near the creek," he suggested. "Shelby mentioned that the tepee was near the creek. There may be a spot over there which Bonsall missed."

They examined the ground carefully but it was evident that the search had been efficient enough. Finally Brannigan shook his head. "They didn't miss anything here — unless it was buried pretty deep."

"It wouldn't have been," she said simply. "There could have been very little time for any kind of digging."

He realized that she was speaking of her mother's tragic end — and possibly of an end to her own hopes of recovering the precious stones. There was resignation in her tone but no sign of hopelessness.

"Shall we ride a little more," he asked, "or is that asking too much after the day's journey?"

"Any reason to go on?" she countered. "This is the spot. If there's nothing here there can be no point in going further."

He shrugged a little. "Purely a selfish idea," he said. "While we're here I have company. When I go back to camp I'm alone again."

"That's a strange statement," she said, frowning. "How do you mean it?"

"The loneliest man in the world is the commander of a small detachment on scout duty. He has no other officer available and discipline forbids him to make companions of his men. Soldiers can enjoy companionship but the officer remains aloof in his regulated dignity and discomfort."

"We'll ride," Karen smiled. "I didn't know I would have to console a hermit."

"Don't laugh," he begged. "It's a very real sort of hermit I am."

"Maybe we should take you into the firm," she laughed. "Tom and I were such lone wolves that we teamed up in self-defense. We didn't know that there was another candidate on hand."

He frowned, then laughed quickly. "I'd accept the invitation," he said — "but I'm afraid your partner would not agree. I didn't understand that it was that kind of a partnership."

"Then you assumed too much about it." Her voice was suddenly sharp but a little troubled. "This is strictly a business proposition."

"I wish I could believe that," he replied soberly. "I'd see what I could do about getting the partnership dissolved. Then I'd make you another offer."

She pulled the roan up abruptly. "Useless," she said, "I think we'd better ask the lieutenant to take us back to camp. We've gone too far."

Halfway through the lazy morning Tom aroused from a restless doze. Doctor Bacon was bantering again in that half complimentary tone of his. This time the reply came in the low, throaty tones of Nan Elson.

"I'm sorry to have deserted you like this, Doctor," she said. "I've been busy with my new boarding house."

"Perfectly all right, my dear," he replied. "You saw us through the emergency nobly enough. We mere men can get along all right now that you and Miss Neilson have us started in the right direction."

"You give us too much credit," she protested.

"No, he don't, ma'am!" a trooper cut in. "We know what you done for us and we won't forget it."

The color came into her cheeks at the praise and Tom realized it was the first time he had ever seen her embarrassed. She tried so hard to maintain her pose of casual sophistication that it worried her to find that men were recognizing her hidden virtues. Now she tried to laugh it off.

"You wouldn't josh a poor widder woman, would you?" she bantered.

Tom recalled that Elson had been dead less than three weeks. Either she was pretty callous about it all or she was simply keeping up her defenses. The hard life of the plains had failed to destroy her beauty; maybe she was determined that neither would it break her spirit. Her pose was her defense against the things she feared.

She passed along between the cots, keeping up a running fire of comment with the various patients, sometimes in general terms but more often with reference to their injuries. Tom could see that she must have done a tremendous amount of work on that first

146

hideous night when amputations and stitching had been in order. Obviously she was familiar with most of the cases.

Presently she stood beside him, her smile quizzical as she met his eyes. "Finally woke up, did you?" she greeted. "We were about ready to sell you for tallow the other night."

He grinned. "I wouldn't suppose you could have noticed me with all the other duties you must have been attending."

"But I did. Often enough so that Miss Neilson was looking daggers at me by morning."

"That's interesting," he commented dryly. "She hasn't seemed very concerned since then."

"Maybe you expect too much."

Again he felt baffled by her attitude. What was she trying to tell him? Her words didn't say much but the look in her eyes seemed to be trying to convey a message.

"How's the boarding house business?" he asked abruptly.

Her smile faded but her tone was still light. "It's a living. One can't be too particular. Some day when you get the ambition you must come over and try one of my meals. Special rates for former patients."

"Set a place for me," he laughed, still trying to fathom her deeper meaning. He felt sure she was trying to tell him something she didn't dare say aloud, probably something about those new men who had come to join Bonsall.

"I'll be expecting you," she said and went on to the next cot.

A week passed drearily enough in the hospital. Twice there was the agony of watching other injured men die. The lesser cases were gradually discharged and gradually the place became less crowded and more wearisome. Jeff was on medical detail most of the time and Shelby noted that the sentries on duty were always troopers from Brannigan's old garrison. Evidently the lieutenant had been telling the truth when he said he was making arrangements for a trustworthy guard. Nevertheless it was irritating for Tom to know that he was having to depend on someone else for his very safety.

Jeff became the regular agent for passing along such news items as came into the post, particularly any reports from Brannigan's party. Patrols were coming and going every day and gradually the word filtered in that Brannigan had left the Moccasin and moved over into White Water Valley. His force had spent only one night in the Moccasin before crossing the ridge and now they were engaged in putting up a cabin on the site of the one which had burned. There was no direct message from either Karen or the lieutenant.

It left Tom to supply the rest of the story from his imagination, something which he did only too well. It would have been bad enough if Karen had gone out there after they had reached a complete understanding. To think of her in company with a big, good-natured Irishman like Brannigan was disturbing, particularly when she might be just annoyed enough to be receptive to his attentions. Brannigan was no fool — and he was certainly human.

The local news was scarcely more comforting. The new men who had joined Bonsall's crew were keeping pretty much to themselves. They didn't show themselves very often around the military post, mostly loafing on the porch of Schwartz's store or riding around the surrounding prairie to kill time.

Jeff kept a pretty good check on them, reporting frequently and in such detail that Tom knew he must be visiting pretty often at the stage station. He said that Nan Elson was about half afraid of them and was keeping to herself as much as possible, only meeting them at meal time. They were mostly tough hombres, according to Jeff. He believed one of them to be a former Quantrell lieutenant and the others were of about the same stripe. Whatever Bonsall was planning he had certainly surrounded himself with a crew that would stop at nothing.

Just a week after Karen's departure Tom was permitted to leave the hospital. The knife wound was healing perfectly while the strains and bruises were just about gone from his neck and shoulder. Ten days, the surgeon had said hopefully, and it seemed that he was going to prove an accurate prophet. He was cheerfully vain about his patient's prompt recovery but it was hard for Tom to share his jubilance. The week had seemed like a year, lying there on his back thinking about a yellow-haired girl who was out in the hills with a personable young lieutenant.

Shelby's first move on leaving the hospital was to visit the trading post. Accompanied by Jeff Speers he walked slowly across the parade ground and entered the store to find Schwartz in conversation with the burly Hogan. Jeff growled a warning at sight of the gunman but Hogan turned with his most disarming grin.

"Good to see you again, Shelby," he greeted. "I'd ha' come over to pass the time o' day with you but I heard you needed rest more 'n anything else. I wanted to explain about that mistake I made in callin' you Brewster. Hope there's no hard feelin's."

Shelby eyed him quietly. The fellow certainly put on a good act of being a big, good-natured scout. Only his known reputation belied the pose. "You don't expect me to feel happy about it, do you?" Tom asked.

Hogan guffawed. "Nope. Just so you ain't real sore. Us fellers gotta work together and we can't afford no feudin' over little things like that."

"Work together? Doing what?"

Hogan's expansive gesture covered practically everything — and nothing. "All kinds of ways. Not enough white men around here for us to fight among ourselves. Maybe you don't know it but I practically saved your life in that there little ruckus up the Moccasin. Just before you went down I picked off one of the varmints what was aimin' to skewer you."

"I don't know about that," Tom said quietly. "I lost track of things after I saw you aimin' in my direction. I sorta figured you was the polecat that shot my horse."

150

He could see Jeff stiffen but Hogan simply laughed again. "Maybe I did at that. It was too fast work for a man to be sure of his shots."

Shelby let it go at that. He felt dead certain that Hogan had tried to kill him — and the slight trace of uneasiness in the man's cackle indicated that Hogan knew he wasn't fooling anybody. One of these days . . .

Jeff cut in with a drawling query. "When do yo' fellers figger to start yore surveyin' business, Ed? Seems like yo' got a mighty big crew eatin' their heads off here in comfort and idleness."

"Mighty soon, suh." Hogan imitated his drawl. "We just had a mite o' delay, suh, beca'se de cap'n, suh, wasn't too dam' pleased with the men I got him — suh."

Tom's quick glance warned Jeff away from the angry move he was about to make. "What's wrong with them, Hogan?" he asked. "Is he afraid a lot of gallows birds won't take to digging as readily as you pilgrims did?"

Hogan laughed again. He seemed to use the laugh to mask his anger and his thoughts just as some people clear their throats or twirl their eyeglasses. "Too bad we didn't find that poor kid's — um — packet, wasn't it?" he said after a moment. "Do you figure she'll manage to get along without it?"

Tom nodded amiably. "She'll be all right," he said. Hogan was fishing. Might as well steer him along a wrong trail. "Nothing in the packet she can't replace when she gets around to it."

"A map maybe?" Hogan asked.

"I didn't say so."

"What else would a woman carry around that would be so valuable? Course, if the kid knows where the — um — mine is she won't need no map."

Tom nodded again. "I didn't say anything about a mine but she'll be all right without the map."

Instantly he knew he had said the wrong thing. He had been amusing himself by misleading Hogan and he had put his foot in it! Whatever crooked land scheme lay back of Bonsall's preparations would surely be passed up for the definite promise of mineral wealth. Already they had passed days and risked their scalps hunting for what they believed to be a map. Now he had aimed them directly at Karen Neilson by implying that she knew the location!

He tried to retrieve his blunder by adding, "Don't let your friend Bonsall waste his time on this deal, Hogan. He can make more out of his crooked preemption graft than he will hunting gold in White Water Valley."

It was a lame addition and Hogan merely grinned. "Nice of you to warn me, partner. Maybe I believe you — and maybe I don't. Anyhow, I reckon we got enough strings to our bows so we won't get plumb ruined on one bad guess."

He swung on his heel and headed for the door, leaving Tom to the bitter realization that he had practically asked for trouble. Under cover of his survey Bonsall could range the hills in search of the imaginary gold strike, leaving his cutthroat tools to their own devices in most of the matter. The easiest method for them — and one that would appeal to them — would

152

be to kidnap Karen Neilson and try to get the information out of her.

Shelby turned to face Schwartz. "Got any idea when that gang figures to start out?" he asked.

The fat trader shrugged. "Purty soon, maybe. Ed chust vanted to know ven I ship der goots east. He said maybe he haf somet'ing to ship if it ain't so soon."

"Make any deal with him?"

"No. Ven I tell him I ship dis veek he says he can't make it."

Tom looked perplexedly at Speers. "Now I wonder what that's all about? If Hogan's shipping anything it's dollars to doughnuts there's something crooked behind it. Jeff, you've got to keep an eye on that mob. If they start for the hills I'll have to duck the surgeon and run for it. I've let Karen in for trouble and I'll have to see that nothing happens to her."

CHAPTER
SIXTEEN

Dan Brannigan had endured a week of tangled emotions. At first it had been a welcome relief from the tedium of garrison duty to be out here in the hills enjoying spring. There was a stern satisfaction in seeing his men laboring at construction work — and liking it. There had been comfort in the report of his scouts that the hills were clear of Indians. Still Brannigan was not happy. There isn't much happiness in being too close to a pretty woman who insists on treating you like an ancient uncle.

He watched her almost sullenly as she stood directing the work of shingling the roof. Three sweating troopers were cutting out shingles, a fourth was passing them up and two others were setting them in place. Karen stood with her hands behind her, feet astride like a man, watching the work. Arms bare to the elbows and her flannel shirt open a bit at the neck, she made a picture which did things to Brannigan's peace of mind. She stirred something within him which he didn't dare show, something which he had to hide from his men as well as the girl.

There had been a certain reserve between them that first evening out of Fort Butler but it had worn off

154

quickly. Karen had evidently been disappointed in her failure to find anything in Moccasin Valley but she quickly recovered her spirits after they pushed on through the burned area and crossed the ridge into White Water Valley.

She had read his intentions when he sent a burial detail ahead and from that moment her attitude had been one of friendly gratitude, a situation which quickly became trying to the man. It brought her closer to him and at the same time erected between them the most complete of barricades.

Now the cabin was just about completed, a sturdy structure which followed the lines of the burned building, even to using the massive stone fireplace which Gunnar Neilson had erected. Brannigan had wanted to build anew, thinking to avoid sad memories for the girl, but she insisted. It was a part of her life, she said, to carry on as her father had begun. She didn't want to forget him.

He walked restlessly across toward the shingle cutters, aware that the men were watching him with some curiosity. It was part of his trouble that his men should thus read his mind. They knew as well as he that their commander was fighting himself. He suspected that they were betting on whether or not he would try to cut Shelby out.

"Looks like we'll be ready to head back for the fort in another day or so," he observed to Sergeant Andrews.

Andrews looked up from his shingle trimming. "I hope there's no hurry, sir. Most of the boys are well enough pleased to be out here in the hills. It's a nice change."

"Sorry, Sergeant. Our orders are to set things up for Miss Neilson and then return immediately. We'll go just as soon as the work is done."

"Yes, sir."

Brannigan turned toward Karen, satisfied that there would be no move from the valley for several days. Andrews would see to it that more jobs were found.

His eyes drank in the full sweep of breast and shoulder as he came up to her. There was a pleasant tan to her neck as she stood with her head back, looking up, and he had a desire to set his lips against that throat. Instead he touched his hat with two fingers and remarked, "You certainly make an excellent foreman. I never saw men work harder or with more enthusiasm."

She met his gaze, ignoring what she found there. "I simply can't thank the army enough," she said simply. "I'm very much ashamed of myself when I remember how I talked about you people. I was pretty bitter about the way my father was treated. I can't see why there is such a difference now."

"That's easy. Your father was a man — looking for help among men who were brought up in a pretty rough school. You are a woman — and a remarkably pretty one."

"Thank you, sir," she laughed. "Perhaps a flatterer like you might be influenced to work by a pretty face but don't tell me my sex caused an old martinet like Major O'Rourke to order this force out! I doubt if he knows whether I'm white or black."

156

"Don't fool yourself about O'Rourke. Maybe he's not as young as he used to be — but he's still Irish. It's a part of his Hibernian sense of humor to order me out here on this job, building a house for you and Shelby when he knows I'd cheerfully cut Shelby's throat to take his place."

She laughed, throwing the wall up between them again. "That's also the Hibernian," she pointed out. "If I didn't know enough to guard against Irish blarney I'd be almost afraid of you. Fortunately I know better. You're just a big, good-hearted Irishman who thinks he has to find some worldly excuse for being as kind as he is. Don't try any more of those fancy gallant speeches, sir!"

"Very clever," he observed dryly. "A woman's 'no' may always mean 'yes', as the poet says, but you certainly stop a man in his tracks with that scornful laugh."

"I certainly didn't mean to be scornful," she assured him. "You have been much too kind for me to feel that way about you — even if I could be so ungrateful."

"Either way I'm out," he grimaced. "I had begun to hope when you seemed so short with Shelby."

"I'm very sorry," she said contritely. "My feeling toward Tom Shelby has no connection with what I might feel toward anyone else."

Brannigan frowned. "Which means I'm not wanted under any circumstances."

"Please! I don't want you to feel that way. I simply have a duty to perform before I can think of anything else. I nearly forgot that duty once . . . but somebody came along to remind me. Now I know my obligation. My personal feelings do not count until this valley has been made into what my father dreamed about."

He stared at her wonderingly, a corner of his mouth twisted into a half smile. "I reckon I'll never understand women," he said half angrily. "I can't make up my mind whether you're just clever or whether you're just about the finest thing I ever missed."

The morning air was still brisk as Shelby walked out across the parade ground. Another day had done wonders for him and he sniffed the varied scents of spring and the post as though every part of it brought pleasure. After a week on his back in the temporary hospital it wasn't hard to find pleasure in everyday objects. All the jelly had gone out of his knees now and he was walking without the body stiffness that had bothered him. Two more days and the knife cut would be well enough for him to risk riding. Then he would make fast tracks for White Water Valley.

The parade ground was deserted, most of the garrison being occupied policing barracks, but Tom knew that something was stirring in the building which still served as quarters for Captain Bonsall. Jeff had passed the word at breakfast. Hogan, Pew and two of the newcomers were going over to see Bonsall.

Tom had almost reached the trading post corner when Bonsall's door opened and Dombrek, the surveyor, came out. The little man seemed angry about something and Tom could see him cursing silently as he stumbled along.

Dombrek kept his eyes on the ground, not seeing Tom until they were only a couple of yards apart. Then Shelby spoke.

"Hello there, my brother ex-convict," he greeted cheerfully. "I see you're still sticking close to the fort where the Indians can't get you."

Dombrek halted with a surprised curse but moved on quickly, speaking to Tom without raising his head. "Go into the trading post and wait for me, will you? I want to talk to you."

"Why not here?" Tom asked as the man went past. "They know we're both jailbirds so it wouldn't ruin anybody's reputation for us to be seen talking together."

Dombrek didn't seem to appreciate the levity. "I'm serious," he said shortly. "Be there in five minutes."

Out of the corner of his eye Tom saw that Bonsall's door was partly open. Someone was watching them. He stared after Dombrek for a moment or two, then turned casually and rounded the corner to the trading post porch.

Schwartz was chewing laboriously at his mustache as he bent over a paper. He looked up with a grunt as Shelby entered. "Halloo, Tommy. Chust in time. Iss der deal der same dis year?"

"Just like before suits me. You see what you can get and take your commission out after deducting expenses. It's the fairest way for both of us."

Schwartz hunched his heavy shoulders slowly, eloquently. "Chust so I know. Day after tomorrow I send der vagon to Sheridan. Not so big a load dis year but —"

"Have you seen the new gunmen Bonsall brought in?" Tom interrupted. "I hear he's got some real killers."

The trader shrugged again. "I don't see any of dem before und I don't see 'em no more, I hope."

He went back to his letter and Tom leaned against the long counter, waiting. It was an odd fact that most of his recent worries had been caused by men he knew slightly or had never seen. Maybe it would be a good idea to push right in on Bonsall's crew and look them over. There had been enough of this loafing around and getting his threats secondhand. He wanted to know whom he had to fight.

Through the side window he could see old man Peters, Schwartz's helper, working on the wheel of a freight wagon. It brought his mind back to the subject of his pelts and he turned to the trader. "I reckon you'd better have my share of this year's proceeds deposited in a good bank back east. Wherever your company banks will do. It will be better that way when I make my cattle deals . . . By the way, how much unnecessary truck did Karen buy? She led me to believe that she had practically bought you out."

Schwartz grinned and fished a list out of a desk drawer. "Smart gal. She don't puy foolish."

Tom glanced at the paper, surprised at the brevity of the list. Two axes, a shovel, two frying pans, two hoes, several kinds of nails, saws, canned goods, matches . . .

160

"Didn't she get anything for herself?" he asked. "I don't see anything here but building materials. What about clothes?"

"She don't puy any. Tommy, I told you she's smart gal. She make plenty clothes ven she's here."

He climbed to his feet as the door opened to admit the furtive figure of George Dombrek. The worried little man turned abruptly to Shelby. "Where can we talk — alone?"

"Right here is all right. Schwartz is safe — and if anyone comes along it won't look so funny. What's up?"

The little man frowned. "Hanged if I know. I came out here to handle a surveying job and it looks like I'm hooked up with some kind of a gang of swindlers. They just chased me out of Captain Bonsall's office and I suspect they're planning some dirty work."

Tom grinned. "I shouldn't be surprised. Have any idea what it is this time?"

Dombrek paced nervously before the counter. "At first I thought it was just a sharp deal on railroad land. Now I'm not sure. Any kind of tramps would do for straw men in a fake settlement graft. Bonsall didn't have to hire men who command gun fighters' wages for this job."

"When is your crew supposed to hit the trail?"

Dombrek shook his head doubtfully. "I don't even know that. I've been ready to leave at any moment. For a while I thought we were being delayed by that Moccasin Valley business. Now I wonder what it's all about."

Tom refused to be baited into disclosing his hand. There was no way of knowing Dombrek's real purpose in this conversation. He might be an honest dupe but he could just as easily be a spy sent to find out how far Shelby's suspicions went.

"You needn't worry," Tom told him easily. "If the land game holds out they'll keep you surveying while the other fellows tend to the gunplay."

The five men in Bonsall's cabin were watching each other with thinly disguised anger. Hogan's grin was as wide as ever but his eyes were narrow as he listened to Bonsall's nasal voice.

"I want it understood," the man was saying, his lips forming a thin line, "that I'm not running any sort of criminal enterprise. My company is willing to spend money in order that we may make a legitimate profit on such land as our asinine lawmakers see fit to give away. American land must be kept for the good of loyal Americans. I'll go to any length to keep our national wealth from getting into the hands of foreigners or those traitors who were so recently in rebellion."

His voice had risen to a peak of intensity as he spoke and Hogan flashed a glance of warning at big Ripper Mulloy. The bulky redhead had robbed both sides without compunction during the war but generally he had claimed to be a patriotic confederate. Hogan didn't want him starting anything with this fanatic who controlled the purse strings.

"We all understand, Captain," he said hastily. "That's why I went to some trouble to find men who won't get

162

soft when we have to take stern measures against the foreign intruders. You're the boss and we're takin' your orders."

"See that you remember that!" Bonsall snapped. "It has been hinted to me that my purpose is suspected. The authorities might cause me a lot of trouble if they get the idea that my crew is doing anything illegal. We must stay within the law!"

"That's the idea," Hogan agreed. "Now how far do we go on this gold mine business?"

Bonsall's face darkened. "We'll go the whole way," he declared harshly. "If there is mineral wealth in these hills I won't see it get into the hands of any but loyal citizens. It is still ours for the taking if we can get it and I shall certainly have no scruples in seeing that neither an immigrant girl nor a dirty rebel ever gets a dirty hand on it!"

Hogan saw that the others were getting restless before this fanaticism and he moved toward the door. "We understand each other all right," he soothed. "When do you figure we oughta get started?"

"Not later than tomorrow! We have been delayed long enough, waiting to see what would come out of this Moccasin Valley business. Tomorrow we go about our business — both parts of it."

It wasn't until they were out of earshot that Hogan ventured a whispered comment to his companions. "Crazy as a bedbug — but we've got to humor him. Play it his way and we'll bide our time. If there's gold up there we'll help him out and see that nobody but us loyal citizens get it."

The others joined in his grin, big Mulloy fingering his guns thoughtfully. His partner, Daniels, just as big as Mulloy and just as dangerous, chuckled aloud. "One bit of gold up there I'd like to get my hands on. I'd sure be willin' to forget my prejudices against foreigners then!"

Hogan's smile disappeared entirely. "One more thing we get straight while we're in the straightenin' business. The girl is mine. Understand?"

Daniels took a belligerent step toward him but Mulloy grabbed his partner's arm. "Hold it, son. This ain't no time to fight about wimmen. Anyhow, I reckon it's about time you and me started workin' on that landlady of ourn. She's takin' an almighty long time to thaw fer a gal as cute as she is."

CHAPTER
SEVENTEEN

It was still a full hour before taps when Jeff found Shelby dozing in a corner of the barracks. A day of restless wandering about the post had made Tom realize his own weakness and he had been glad to find a quiet spot to rest in. A card game was in progress across the big room but there were no soldiers within earshot as Jeff approached.

The lanky trooper's face was dead serious as he settled himself beside Shelby. "Got time to be bothered with my pet troubles?" he asked.

Tom looked up, surprised at the tone. "What troubles?" he asked with a smile. "I never thought you had any troubles as long as they didn't have your ornery carcass in a calaboose somewhere."

Speers acknowledged the pleasantry with a brief grin. "Maybe not troubles exactly. Jest a question or two. I want to talk to you about Nan Elson."

"That's nice. So I'm a sympathetic shoulder for you young fellers to lean on now, am I? Well, spring does funny things to the male animal. Fire away. I know what the feeling's like."

"I'm serious," Jeff protested. "I like the gal a heap — and sometimes I get the idea she's right fond of me.

The trouble is I can't quite figger her out. My 'listment's up this week and I was kinda figgerin' on havin' a try at that stage company job. Since Elson was shot — drivin' another man's trip — there ain't been no regular man at the station. Nan has been runnin' things with that half-breed of Dutchy's to help her. If I thought her and me could get along I'd make her a proposition."

Tom chuckled. "Now that's real romantic of you! Are you aiming to marry the girl or the stage company?"

"You're a fine one to talk! You and your partnership with the purtiest blonde what ever come west of the Big Muddy! I'm figurin' two ways. This stage station stands a chance to be a good business spot if the railroad comes through. A man could make a nice thing of it if he had a woman like Nan Elson to help him along. Trouble with me is I don't want it to be like that. I ain't askin' no gal to marry me 'til I'm sure I won't be sorry afterwards."

"You don't want much," Tom told him dryly. "You're asking for a sure thing in the biggest lottery ever run. What makes you think she'll have you — and how come you're not sure you want her?"

Jeff squirmed uncomfortably. "I never was much of a hand with women. I ain't goin' around proposin' unless I'm danged sure I mean it. If she wants to throw me out when I ask her — that's up to her. Whether I ask her or not is up to me. I figured maybe you could give me a bit of advice, seein' as how you seem to understand her so good."

166

Tom looked to see if he could detect any added meaning in the remark but Jeff was serious. "You've got me plenty wrong on that count," Tom told him. "I've about made up my mind that I don't understand anything about any woman — particularly Karen and Nan."

"But you do," Jeff persisted. "Every time you talk to her both of you seem to be understanding a lot of things you never say out loud. For a spell I was downright worried about you because you and Nan seemed to savvy each other so good. Then I decided it was jest one o' them cases where folks are so much alike they can read each other's thoughts. That's why I want you to give me your opinion."

Shelby regarded his friend in amazement. "You philosopher!" he exclaimed. "Maybe you've got something there. I enjoy talking to Nan but I certainly don't feel the same way about her that I do about Karen. She puzzles me but I guess it's just because I try to fit her into some regular pattern. If I take her as I find her she makes sense."

"What kind of sense?"

"Good sense. My guess is that she has had a good home behind her but left it because of some sort of misunderstanding. I figure she tried to get away from her troubles and found out that you can't run away like that. Somehow she found herself out here in the West. She didn't like things as she found them but she had learned her lesson about running from things she didn't like. She has been fighting to play the game and still not let this life beat her into something she doesn't want to be."

Jeff frowned thoughtfully, minutes passing before he finally remarked, "I don't know how you came up with all that tea leaves business but it's what I hoped you'd say."

"I don't think I'm far wrong about her. She's down and out or she wouldn't have taken in those boarders — but has anybody heard her complain? To see her you'd think she didn't have a worry on earth. She's pretty much all right, if you're asking me."

"I asked you," Jeff said, standing up. "Now I'm goin' over there and pop the question. Want to walk out a piece and get some air?"

"Just across the parade ground," Tom laughed. "I'm not going to go hold your hand while you speak your piece."

"You're dang right you ain't! I got no way of tellin' how she feels about you. Maybe she thinks because you and her understand each other that you're souls made for each other. Gals are some peculiar that way and a homely galoot like me can't stand much competition."

Tom had wondered about Nan Elson's feelings but he would have been the last one to mention it. Already the subject had caused enough trouble with Karen acting as she had. He covered his momentary confusion by stooping to reach under the cot for his gun belt. "An ounce of prevention . . ." he quoted, strapping on the weapon.

168

"It's a dark night and there's polecats on this post would admire to finish a job they didn't manage to handle before."

There was a light in the front room of the stage company's building but Jeff ignored it, leading the way toward the back door. "Nan blocked off a room for herself," he explained. "I helped her board up the doorway before she took them rannies to board."

Tom halted, preparatory to turning back. "A good idea," he commented. "I wouldn't trust one of those —"

He stopped abruptly as the sound of a brief scuffle came from the back room of the stage station. A man cursed sharply and another male voice rasped a guarded warning.

Jeff dashed forward with a grunt of anger. Shelby was close behind as the lanky trooper jerked without result at the door latch, then hurled his spare frame against the barrier. The door burst open before the fury of his assault and Tom followed him into the lamplit room.

Directly in front of them big Ripper Mulloy was digging for his gun while beside them and partly behind the door Dirk Daniels struggled to subdue Nan Elson. Tom had a quick flash of the woman's angry face behind Daniels' bleeding hand, then he moved into action as Jeff swerved to drive at Daniels.

Mulloy's gun had already cleared leather but he had evidently intended to fire at Speers. The instant of hesitation gave Tom the chance to make his play. He moved with a speed that surprised him, bringing his gun up just as Mulloy swung to meet the new

169

antagonist. He felt a jerk at his left hip as his .44 bucked against his palm, the lamp flickering sharply under the double concussion. Then a body slammed against his tender ribs, catching him off balance and knocking the gun out of his hand.

He knew that his shot had felled Mulloy but the rest of the picture was not so clear. All he could be sure of was that he was on the floor, trying to recover his Colt before the burly Daniels could reach it. Waves of pain were sweeping through the injured side and he was fighting a double battle, the struggle with Daniels and the fight to retain consciousness. He didn't know what had happened to Jeff or Nan Elson. For the moment he didn't have time to think about it very much or even to care.

His fingers were closing over the butt of the Colt just as Daniels crashed down against him, sending red waves of agony through his whole body. He was conscious of one final, desperate struggle, then Daniels seemed to collapse beside him. Tom's hand closed on the gun but the lamplight faded before he could draw it toward him.

He fought doggedly against the blackness and when things began to take shape again he knew that he had been out only a matter of seconds. Mulloy still lay where he had fallen. Daniels groaned on the floor and Jeff Speers was climbing painfully to his knees.

Tom rolled to a sitting position before he saw Nan. She was standing over him unsteadily, careless of the picture she made. The upper half of her dress had been torn almost completely away and she still gripped the back of a shattered chair.

"Are you hit?" she asked breathlessly.

It was difficult for Tom to concentrate on an answer to that question. Her concern was so apparent that he felt a quick dread of what she might do. Her eyes were fixed anxiously upon him, the deeper expression in them something he could not quite understand.

Across the room he saw that Jeff was watching tensely. Suddenly the vast ache in his side meant no more to him than did the fallen outlaw at his feet. The important thing was that Nan Elson should not spoil everything by making a bad move. He couldn't let Jeff be hurt now!

He let his left hand drop to his hip, the fingers encountering the scraps of ragged leather where Mulloy's hasty slug had carried away cartridge loops and a couple of .44 shells. "Nary a scratch," he said hastily. "Looks like you swing a mighty nasty chair. Thanks for the help." He tried to make it sound casual but he knew his acting wasn't very convincing.

There was a queer light of amusement in her eyes as she turned away, almost as though she had read the fear in him and had found humor in the discovery. Surrounded by death and violence she could still laugh at a man who had been afraid of her advances. Tom felt oddly resentful but not for very long. She was already helping Jeff to his feet, one arm around him even as she worked with her free hand to repair some of the damage to her dress. Something in the way she was looking at the trooper brought quick satisfaction to

Shelby. It was humbling to have her laugh at him the way she had done — but under the circumstances it was a great relief.

Running footsteps sounded outside and Tom backed painfully away from the sagging door, placing himself so that he could cover the doorway and still keep an eye on Daniels. Now that the fight had started it would be a pleasure to throw lead into some of the rest of these crooks!

Then a blue uniform appeared in the opening and Tom holstered his gun. The guard had appeared and more soldiers were coming up behind him. Sudden relief made Tom aware of the pain in his side. The army was on hand and could take over; he could afford to admit the nausea which had gripped him since Daniels' attack.

He managed to find a seat on a bench but after that he didn't pay much attention to the rush of events. He knew that an officer had arrived to take charge. He watched a detail carry out the dead body of Mulloy. He knew that the officer was asking questions of the groggy Daniels. Then Daniels was taken away under guard. Nan Elson was telling her story to the officer, making a hero of Tom Shelby but keeping mighty close to Jeff Speers. After that the whole scene became confused and Tom knew he was being carried over to the barracks. Two or three times he heard Doctor Bacon scolding as he worked, a familiar sound which helped put him to sleep.

The clamor of reveille brought him to his senses, sore but feeling little the worse for the fight. Jeff was standing near the doorway, his grin anticipating the news he wanted to tell.

"Feel good enough to hear a sad item, Reb?" he asked. "Your old school chum Bonsall is leavin' the post — by request. Major O'Rourke got on his high horse last night after he heard Captain Bent's report. They held an inquiry about midnight and Bonsall got his walkin' papers. Either he has his crowd outa the post by daylight or they all go into the jug. They're leavin' now."

Tom worked himself to a sitting position, vastly relieved to find that though his side was sore he was not crippled. "I'll have to see this," he chuckled. "Doctor Bacon will probably cuss me out but it'll be worth it."

Jeff lent him a supporting arm as they crossed to a window. "Doc won't mind. He told me last night you was too dumb to get hurt much. Daniels just jarred you when he smashed against the ribs; he didn't bust you up any."

Tom nodded.

"What about you and the fair widder? Did you get everything fixed up?"

"You bet your boots! She's the greatest little . . ."

"Ah, Spring! What it will do to you kids!"

"Rats!" Jeff was very red but he wasn't letting it stop him. "You're just as bad only it ain't quite so new to you."

Tom changed the subject. "What happened last night? All I remember straight is swapping shots with Mulloy. I saw him go down and then Daniels hit me. It seemed like I spent a couple of hours scrambling for my gun with him trying to get there first. What were you doing all that time? Kissing the widow?"

Speers wrinkled his nose disgustedly. "I was a sucker. When I went for Daniels he let go of Nan and caught me foul with a knee. He was divin' into you before I even hit the floor. The next thing I knew Nan was clubbin' him over the head with a chair. The whole thing didn't last half a minute and I watched most of it from the floor. You and Nan did all the scrappin'."

Tom frowned soberly. "I don't know whether I'd want to be in your boots — falling for a woman who uses chairs like that! Imagine having to spend the rest of your life dodging chairs! For one thing the cost of chairs would just about ruin a man."

"Shut up and look. There's the guard marchin' the prisoners outa the stage station. I reckon Hogan and Pew musta worked all night gettin' ready. All the others were under guard."

In the half light of morning Tom could distinguish the forms of the original four. Bonsall and Dombrek sat their horses sullenly near the barracks, pack animals laden with the surveyor's instruments close beside them. They seemed to be holding aloof from the others, Bonsall angry and Dombrek fearful. Hogan and Pew had taken command of the detachment and were getting their men outfitted.

Bonsall was still wearing a uniform coat but the guards apparently took no notice of him or his rank. No officers of the garrison appeared on the scene, a sergeant from Bent's troop handling the business.

The bulky form of Daniels loomed large in the crowd of surly outlaws. Both the man and his horse were big enough to attract attention but it was his bandaged head which caught Shelby's eye. The flash of white gave him almost as much satisfaction as the angry fidgeting of Bonsall. It was pleasant to see these scoundrels being driven from the fort but there was a serious flaw in the pleasure. From here their business would take them into the hills where Karen might even now be alone. That thought could not be a happy one, whichever way the situation stood. Either Karen was out there alone and in danger or she was out there in the dangerous company of Dan Brannigan.

Jeff's nudge disturbed the train of doleful thought. "You want to watch that Daniels gent," he warned. "Last night he swore he'd get hunk with you for killin' Mulloy. The lanky Swede next to him was Mulloy's man too. If you meet either of 'em in the hills you want to be lookin' at 'em over a gun barrel!"

Shelby nodded silently. After a moment he asked, "How about lending me a hand today, Jeff? I want to leave this evening instead of waiting 'til morning. Schwartz will take care of shipping the pelts and I don't want to delay any longer in getting out there into the valley. I can't forget that I gave Hogan a steer which will aim him directly at Karen."

Doctor Bacon's voice interrupted sharply from behind them. "Speers! If you're on hospital detail you'll get that man into his cot immediately! He won't ride out of this post for another two days if I have to put a guard over him!"

Jeff saluted briskly. "Yes, sir. I just caught him at the window and I was tryin' to get him back to bed."

The surgeon grinned at Jeff's owlish innocence. "Shelby," he said severely, "I don't know whether you've got the most to fear from your friends or your enemies. With the help you're getting from your partners you'll probably kill yourself before you get away from here!"

CHAPTER
EIGHTEEN

Shelby fretted helplessly on his cot throughout the long, sunshiny day. It was the sort of weather which made him think of cattle browsing through the valleys in search of new green, the sort of day when a man could work with energy and cheerfulness. Today he should be out there in the valley getting ready to make a ranch out of hopes and plans; instead he was flat on his back and actually under guard. Doctor Bacon wasn't taking chances on his reluctant patient.

The irony of it would have been funny if it had not been so irritating. Army life and army discipline had meant a lot of trouble to Tom Shelby but it had never been quite like this before. As a prisoner of war and later as a converted Rebel he had known the harsh discipline of officers who feared and distrusted him. Now he was under the restraint of men who wanted to take care of him because they liked him. It was a queer twist but it still put him in the position of having to take orders which irked him.

Just before dusk a messenger came in, reporting that Lieutenant Brannigan's detail was still in White Water Valley. Their work was about completed but they were showing no intention of returning. Doctor Bacon brought the news to Tom, apparently hopeful that the information would ease the strain. What he didn't foresee was the way Shelby would interpret Brannigan's motive.

"Lucky for you we need a base for our scouts in the hills," he told Shelby.

"There hasn't been any sign of Indians for weeks now but the major isn't taking any chances. You'll be out there before he calls in the outpost."

Tom couldn't work up any enthusiasm on the subject. An impatient man on a hospital cot isn't likely to be very reasonable, particularly when he has to keep hoping for something he fears. He wanted Brannigan to stay in the valley — yet he feared what might happen there.

Another dawn saw the departure of Dutchy's freight wagon for the railhead at Sheridan. Tom watched from the barracks window, gambling that Doctor Bacon would come in and catch him. The load wasn't so big this season. His own stack of pelts made up fully half of the shipment, very few trappers having come in from the hills. Indian troubles during the winter had put a crimp in the trapping business and Tom knew the fact was in his favor. A short market would mean better than average prices.

The heavy wagon rumbled off along the stage trail, the two nondescript figures on the seat paying scant attention to the final shouts of their rotund employer. They didn't need Dutchy Schwartz to tell them how to drive a freight wagon — and that was all they needed to know. Theirs was simply the task of getting the load to

178

Sheridan. Schwartz's company would see to marketing the furs and sending back the necessary trade goods for the post.

Tom heaved a sigh of relief as he went back to his cot. Now that the trails were clear of Indians there was little risk of loss. In a matter of a couple of weeks Schwartz would get word by mail as to the amount deposited to Shelby's credit. Then the cattle drive could come along any time. The cattleman might have made a deal for diamonds but he would take money when he found that the gems were gone. Barring serious troubles in the valley the ranch business was at last beginning to get under way.

At noon Doctor Bacon released his impatient charge. "Take it easy this afternoon and maybe we'll let you go in the morning. That fight never helped your condition any but it doesn't seem to have caused any serious complications. Don't overdo it and don't try to ride too hard tomorrow."

Tom wasted no time in heading for the trading post. He could use the afternoon in completing his preparations and would be ready to ride out at dawn. There was no time to be lost. Brannigan might leave White Water Valley any time now and it wouldn't be very long until Bonsall's outfit would be making their calls there.

He found Schwartz alone in the store but they had no sooner begun to talk business when Mrs. Elson arrived. Her smile held some of its customary challenge but there was a new light in her eyes now. "I saw you come in," she explained, "and I had to come over to tell

179

you how much I appreciate what you did for me. I would have come to tell you at the barracks but Jeff wouldn't hear of it. He said you needed rest more than you needed thanks. I almost believe the man is jealous."

Tom laughed. "He should be. Any fellow who wouldn't be jealous of you wouldn't be worthy of having you."

"But you didn't want him to be too jealous, did you?" she asked significantly, her smile reminiscent of the look she had given him just before she had turned to help Jeff.

He grinned sheepishly but retorted, "I didn't want him to be jealous of me. That would have been a mistake."

"You're not very flattering now," she complained. "And after making such a nice start, too!"

"You know what I mean — just as you always do. Somehow you and I understand each other too well. You're a mighty attractive woman but I'd sure hate to think of living with you for very long. It would be too much like living in a glass cage with nothing in front of my eyes but a mirror. My thoughts would never have any privacy and all I'd ever see would be my own ideas coming back at me."

She laughed merrily. "Exactly. I'd be in the same fix — and a woman loses most of her effectiveness if she can't retain a bit of mystery about her."

Schwartz had been scratching his head in fine perplexity at this odd conversation but now he broke in to announce the arrival of the afternoon stage. Mrs. Elson flashed Tom a quick smile and rushed out, anxious to oversee the change of teams. Tom grinned to see that it was Jeff who was doing the work, apparently well on his way to taking over the new job he had talked about.

The stage brought no passengers to Fort Butler and Shelby was going on with his buying when Jeff came in, a trace of uneasiness showing in his eyes.

"Wasn't your drivers figgerin' to follow the stage line, Dutchy?" he asked.

"Ja. Vhy?"

"Stage driver claims he ain't seen hide nor hair of any wagon along the trail."

Shelby and the trader bolted for the door without a word. There was only the single poorly marked trail across the rolling prairie to Fort Wallace and Sheridan. If the freight wagon was not on that trail there could be but one possible reason.

The stage driver could tell them nothing more than Jeff had already reported. He hadn't been taking any particular note of the trail but he had been alert enough so that he could never have missed seeing a wagon. Yes, he might have missed the sign where a wagon had turned off. All he knew was that there hadn't been an eastbound wagon this side of Fort Wallace.

The morning had seemed endless but the afternoon was worse. A squadron of Bent's men under Lieutenant Gordon were ordered out on the trail of the missing vehicle but Tom didn't manage to accompany them. Both Major O'Rourke and Doctor Bacon vetoed his proposal, arguing that there was no reason for him to risk his recovery by making such a ride when there might be no real reason for it. He let them persuade him but it was torture to wait around and wonder. If anything had happened to that wagon it would mean the wrecking of a whole winter's work.

He tried to calculate the probable cost of the herd Karen expected. She had been uncertain as to its size and the nature of the payment gave no hint as to price. He could only go by her general impression that the drive would be a sizeable one. If it turned out to be very big it would completely wreck his savings, leaving nothing for the inevitable expenses which would be part of the work of building up a brand-new spread. Still he had to make every effort to handle the cattle deal; it wouldn't do to force some other man with capital into becoming a competitor. There wasn't enough free land in this area to support too many spreads.

There was still a chance that the Neilson diamonds might be recovered but he couldn't count on that. The lack of any message from Karen made him fairly certain that no discovery had been made. One way or another he didn't want to figure on stocking the ranch that way. He wanted to use his own resources, not those of the girl. The partnership idea was all right but he wasn't keen on letting Karen put up the capital. Poor business, no doubt, but a matter of pride.

He worked doggedly throughout the afternoon, hopeful that matters would turn out all right so he could leave in the morning as planned. It was just possible that a pair of salty old citizens like Peters and

182

the breed would have taken a short cut somewhere. The stage line was far from straight and they would know of alternate routes if anyone did.

By nightfall he was pretty well exhausted. It hurt his pride to acknowledge his own weakness but there was a compensation: his physical exhaustion allowed him to sleep instead of lying awake worrying.

Nan Elson was living at the stage station again so Tom moved into the room she — and Karen before her — had occupied at the trading post. It gave him a chance to get some early evening rest away from the noise of the barracks and it would be handy for an early morning departure — if such proved possible.

He fell asleep almost as soon as he crawled into the bunk. It seemed only an instant later that he was awakened by the glimmer of a lantern in the room. Jeff Speers, fully dressed, was carrying the light while Dutchy Schwartz in a voluminous flannel nightshirt stood beside him.

"Feel well enough to ride, Reb?" Speers asked. "Looks like there's a job to do."

Shelby came up quickly, ignoring the soreness of his ribs and the stiffness of softened leg muscles. "What's wrong?" he demanded.

"Lieutenant Gordon's outfit rode in just before midnight. They found the freight wagon in a gulley about a half mile from the stage trail. Dutchy's men and the mules had been shot. The pelts are all gone. Trail cuts northwest toward the foothills. The boys figure the load was hauled away on pack animals. Four riders and four led horses."

Tom swore aloud as he pulled on his pants. "Why didn't they follow the trail?" he demanded. "There's no place in the hills for bandits to dispose of pelts. If Gordon's men had stuck to their sign they might have caught them before they could get clean away."

Jeff shrugged. "Nobody in the outfit was much of a tracker, I reckon. They had orders to find the wagon and report. They did just that — and brought in the bodies of Peters and the breed. Now the major wants to know if you're fit to take a detail and go after the killers."

"How soon do we leave?"

"Soon as you're ready. We let you sleep 'til we figured it was near time to start. No use gettin' there while it's still dark."

Tom was already gathering up his equipment. "How many men in the detail? No use trying to pack an army around the country if we hope to get anywhere."

Jeff grinned. "Just four of us. Coulter, Barstow, Yerg and me. You remember Coulter and Yerg from the day they dumped you in the calaboose, I reckon. They figure this is likely part of the same scrap so they want in. Barstow was a pal of old man Peters and he wants a crack at the dirty bushwhackers what killed him. I told the major you'd rather have four volunteers like that than a half company."

"Right. How about getting the pinto saddled for me while I'm finishing up here? He's had lots of rest and ought to be good for a hard chase."

"Sure you don't want a cavalry horse?"

"No. It's my chore and I'll use my own horse for it. Maybe the pinto will be luckier for me than he was for his old Oglala boss."

"He better be! Get a move on. Mrs. Schwartz is gettin' you some grub but don't try to eat all your hide will hold now. It's three hours to daylight and if we start pronto we'll be there as soon as you can see to track. Another lot of troopers will go out at dawn to pick up the wagon."

CHAPTER
NINETEEN

Jeff's timing proved accurate. The sun hadn't yet appeared above the long rolls of eastern prairie when the five men halted beside the empty freight wagon. Night prowling coyotes had torn at the carcasses of the mules but otherwise the scene was just about as Lieutenant Gordon had reported leaving it. The troopers had covered any tracks which might have been made around the wagon but the trail toward the hills was clear.

"The bandits shot Peters and the breed from ambush back there at that line of cottonwoods," Jeff suggested. "Then they drove the wagon out here where they could load without bein' seen from the trail. They musta shot the mules just before they left."

Tom nodded a silent agreement and led the way along the confused trail which Gordon's men had followed. Within a mile they could see where the troopers had cut back to carry out their orders. After that Tom had a chance to study the sign, hopeful of learning something of the men he had to catch.

Obviously Lieutenant Gordon had been right about their number. Four riders, each leading a single pack animal. Just enough pack horses to handle the load.

Was that a coincidence or had the thieves planned it well?

All of the horses were shod, bearing out the impression Tom had gained when he failed to spot any moccasin tracks around the wagon. The bandits were not Indians.

None of the pursuers had uttered a word since striking the unobscured trail but after a mile of steady travel Shelby pointed to the ground. "Notice the size of that set of prints on the right. It took a lot of horse to make those tracks!"

Jeff met his glance understandingly. "Biggest hoss I've seen around here lately was the big bay Daniels was forkin' when he left the post the other mornin'. I reckon maybe Coulter's guess was right about who pulled this job."

"I'd bet on it! Whoever planned this not only knew about the wagon going through today but they knew how big a load was on it. They waited in ambush. Peters and the Indian never had a chance."

Jeff nodded. "And Hogan went to a bit of trouble to ask Schwartz about when the wagon was goin'."

"Right. Hogan planned it. Daniels is with him. I wonder if Bonsall had a hand in the game or whether this is just overtime work for the boys?"

Trooper Barstow, a silent individual whose sorrowful countenance masked a brisk fighting spirit, grunted something that was almost a chuckle. "My guess is Bonsall don't even know about it. I'd pick that big Swede as one of these skunks. Him and Daniels was plenty sore when they rode out of the fort. I was helpin' herd them out and they was cussin' you plenty. Swore they'd get square for the killin' of Mulloy."

"Sounds reasonable," Tom agreed quietly. "The fourth hombre is probably Ike Pew. What I can't make out is why they're headin' for the hills. There's nothing in this direction short of the Union Pacific line into Denver — and that's plenty of ride through Sioux country."

"It's a dodge," Coulter suggested. "They'll double back and strike for some place where they can turn the plunder into cash."

Tom shook his head. "It don't look like it to me. They're heading straight for the hills. Last I knew there wasn't any kind of settlement in this direction."

"We're headin' square fer the mouth of Alder Crick," Yerg put in. "I been up this way before. Alder's a shorter valley than most, a sort of a blind alley that fetches up all of a sudden."

Tom frowned thoughtfully, scanning the hills before them. "I reckon this is the thumb side," he mused, half to himself.

He saw Jeff's look of wonder and grinned. "No, I'm not out of my head. I was just thinking about a way I had of mapping this country."

He held out his right hand, his mind going back to that afternoon in White Water Valley when he had used the device to show Karen their situation. "White Water Valley is the gap between my first and second fingers. Moccasin Valley runs between the second and third, the stage line coming next. That makes Alder the thumb side of the first finger."

188

Yerg laughed. "Right enough. By the looks of things right now we'll have to chase them polecats clear up yore arm into the mountains."

There was a general chuckle but relaxation in the grimness on each face. These men were ready for even such a chase as that. Only Shelby himself knew how much the ride had already taken out of him. Ten days in the hospital was no way to train for a job like this.

At midday they were working into the rolling country which marked the beginnings of Alder Creek's short valley. Jeff had ceased to watch the trail now. He was riding close beside Shelby, keeping an anxious eye on his friend. It galled Tom to know that his weakness was so apparent but he kept silent, too weary to dissemble. Several times he almost lost his stirrups, his legs having gone numb almost as soon as the injured side began to ache. Still he ignored all hints for a rest.

They approached the stream at a long angle and the trail disappeared into the water. Coulter swore excitedly as they halted. "Here's where they do it!" he snapped. "I figured all along they'd double back. They went into the crick so it'll look like they're goin' on up, then they cut back and headed for a settlement to sell their loot."

Tom smiled faintly. Once more he was being reminded of Karen. She had resorted to much the same trick in covering their trail into the little glen where they had camped. Somehow he didn't believe that was the explanation here. These men weren't doubling back after so long a ride. They must have some plan which involved a return to Bonsall's camp along the stage line.

"We'll see pretty quick," he said. "This creek's too small for eight men to use it and not make some kind of a trail."

He headed the pinto upstream to where a cottonwood had toppled into the creek, partially blocking it. "Take a look out there, Jeff," he suggested. "They never took four pack horses over that log without leaving some kind of a mark."

Jeff slid from his saddle and worked his way out on the log. "Plenty of sign," he grinned. "Even I can see it. Hoofs took some nicks outa the log and the moss is scraped offa the rocks on the bottom. They went this way, all right."

He looked anxiously at Shelby as he came back to the bank, then suddenly he announced, "We'll rest a bit here. The ponies need a breather — and so do I. Climb down, you saddle polishers! Time for grub."

Tom didn't find the strength to protest. The others were already on foot and he slid awkwardly from the saddle, his knees buckling under him as he hit the ground.

Jeff took the pinto's bridle. "Stay right down there, Reb," he advised. "Stretch out and don't bat an eyelash 'til we're ready to move again."

Tom didn't need the injunction. An overpowering weariness gripped him and his eyes closed in spite of his best efforts.

The brief nap brought back some of his spent strength but he discovered that his weary muscles had stiffened most painfully. Under Jeff's urging he managed to swallow a bit of the food Barstow had been

190

packing, then he staggered toward his horse. "Got to keep moving," he said grimly. "We'll never catch them by sitting around here."

Jeff boosted him into the saddle without replying. The lanky trooper was worried but he knew that it would be useless to talk about any more rest now.

They pushed ahead, straight into the afternoon sun until they were fairly between the rising ridges which Tom had identified as thumb and index finger. It was new country to him but he saw that it was much the same as the valleys to the south. Not so broad as the White Water or the Moccasin but the same kind of range country.

Five miles from the point where they had halted, four and a half from the spot where the trail had come out on dry ground again, they found the sign bearing off to the south and entering a little notch which appeared in the low ridge.

"So this is the way of it!" Tom observed. "A pass through into White Water. They're headed back for Bonsall's camp, all right!"

"Wouldn't it be a shame if they'd run into Brannigan's boys?" Jeff grinned.

Coulter grunted pessimistically. "No such luck. Hogan knows about Brannigan. He'll give that part of the valley a wide berth."

Tom didn't speak the thought which forced itself into his mind. Suppose Brannigan was no longer at the Neilson place? It would be an excellent opportunity for Hogan to kill two birds with one stone. His pelt stealing expedition could quite handily be made to cover the kidnapping of Karen.

The notch was not a long one and within a half hour they were in White Water Valley. No part of the country seemed familiar to Shelby yet. His only previous experience with it had been the night when he and Karen had passed through on their flight to Fort Butler. It had been dark then and he had seen nothing of this lower end. Naturally he had not been aware of the cross notch which connected with Alder.

The robbers' trail swung upstream, no other fresh sign appearing in the valley. Jeff was inclined to cheer at this circumstance, reasoning that it indicated Brannigan's continued presence at the Neilson place.

"We've got 'em in the pinchers," he crowed. "Keep an eye skinned; they may cut back when they find they've got some of our boys ahead of 'em."

Tom refused to be cheered. He was too bone weary to feel confident about anything and he realized there were other reasons for the lack of sign. "We'll keep a sharp lookout," he agreed — "but we can't be sure of Brannigan. He might have gone back to Moccasin Valley before heading toward the fort. After all, his official business out here was to serve as an outpost for the major."

Speers didn't comment on the way Tom had stressed the word "official". Instead he asked, "What time of day do you figure the polecats passed here?"

"Toward dusk last evening. That's another reason why I'm not too hopeful of finding them in a trap. They knew about Brannigan's camp here and they could have slipped by it in the dark, keeping to the north side of the valley."

The trail was clear now and Coulter rode out ahead, acting as an advance guard while Yerg and Speers rode beside Shelby. It was evident to all of them that Tom was sticking to his saddle by main force of will, determined to learn of Karen's situation before he would surrender to the pain and weariness which all but overpowered him.

Presently they struck a broader stretch of valley and Tom noticed familiar landmarks. This was the flatland he had picked for his home ranch, good pasturage with some excellent meadowland. He and Karen had crossed it in the fading hours of daylight before their night ride.

The sight of it helped him to a new effort. "This looks better," he observed. "I know where I am now. A mile ahead there's a stretch of timber covering the valley floor. After that the valley narrows sharply but spreads out again into the basin Neilson picked for a homestead. If Hogan had doubled back away from Brannigan we'd have met him long before this."

Even as he spoke he saw that Coulter had reined up and was looking back. The trooper pointed ahead as they came up with him. "Our bushwhackin' friends camped here last night. There's the ashes of their fire. Either they felt mighty safe to stop like this or they wanted to know more about Brannigan's camp before they went on."

The others held back and Tom went forward to read sign. He could see plenty without leaving the saddle so he did not dismount. He was afraid he wouldn't be able to mount again if he once found himself on the ground.

"They stayed all night," he said after some study of the spot. "See where they rolled their soogans by the fire. The horses were picketed between the fire and the creek. We're only about ten hours behind them now."

"Fair enough," Coulter growled. "Even if they slipped past our boys in the early mornin' there's still a chance. Fresh men and fresh horses can take up the hunt soon."

Shelby didn't reply. Too many things might have happened just ahead for him to be making any confident predictions. He urged the pinto forward but Coulter pushed by him to take the lead again. Obviously the troopers had reached some sort of an understanding and they were trying to make him save his energy for the last couple of miles.

The trail continued into the woodland and after a short distance Coulter halted again, waiting for Shelby to come up. "Your turn again, tracker," he grunted. "Looks to me like there was some kind of a powwow here and then the devils split up. Only two sets of tracks on the other side of this brook so I reckon the others took to the water."

Once more Tom forced his weary senses to the task of reading sign. "You called your shot," he said briefly. "Two men crossed. Neither one was Daniels. That means Daniels and another man went downstream with the pack horses."

"How do you know they didn't go upstream?" Yerg asked.

194

"I don't. I'll bet the other way, though. This brook comes from a mountain spring only a short distance back. There's nothing there but an enclosed glen with no way out on the other side. My guess is they went down this brook to White Water Creek and used the creek to detour around Brannigan's camp."

"Then we push on," Coulter said. "Yerg and me will take to the brush and try to pick up any trail along the crick. The rest of you ride on 'til you meet Brannigan's fellows. How far away is the Neilson place?"

"Less than a mile. If you don't find anything along the stream in that distance you'd better cut back to meet us. No telling what we'll find ahead."

CHAPTER
TWENTY

The weary horses seemed to sense the journey's end. Shelby's tough little paint moved out so energetically that Jeff reached across to pull him down. It was all too evident that Tom was in no condition for any hard riding and Jeff wasn't taking any chances on a fall.

They pushed on through the woodland where Shelby had first found Karen. He thought he could distinguish the cluster of young pines where she had been standing when he launched his attack but he could not be certain. In the late afternoon sun the forest looked completely different from the sodden woodland he recalled so well. Then their chances of escape had appeared slim indeed . . . but they had gotten through. Maybe he could hope for an equally fortunate ending to the present complication of troubles.

Presently the forest thinned out and they could see blue-clad figures in the clearing ahead, men who worked around cooking fires. It was a cheering sight for men who had scarcely dared hope for such good fortune. Brannigan's force was still in camp. That meant Karen was safe.

Tom was holding to his saddle horn with both hands now, the feeling of relief leaving him weaker than ever.

No longer did he have to keep himself erect by sheer force of desperation. Help was in sight.

Shouts greeted them from the camp and they could see Karen at the door of the cabin. She still wore the flannel shirt and buckskin breeches which she had donned for the ride. The clothes didn't look so new now. They showed the stains of hard work but they still set off her slim figure in a way which brought memories — and hopes.

Brannigan was coming across from the far side of camp, his appearance bringing other memories to the weary man on the pinto. Karen was safe — but for whom? Had the girl allowed her pique to turn her toward Brannigan? The uncertainty helped to kill a large part of the satisfaction Tom had felt at finding the camp.

He drove the thought from his mind, concentrating on the matter of more immediate concern. He had to make certain that Brannigan understood the situation clearly and would take up the pursuit. The thieves must be caught before they could make good their escape.

They halted at the outer edge of the camp, a pair of troopers coming up quickly to take the horses. The move told Shelby how utterly weary he must seem; these men would never have presumed to handle his mount if the circumstances hadn't made the service so obviously needed.

He forced himself to the effort of getting a numb leg over the saddle but the result wasn't very good. Jeff and a trooper caught him to keep him from falling but he slumped between them, unable to put any weight on his rubbery legs. "Better let me down, boys," he said grimly. "I can talk just as well on the ground — and I'll sure feel better."

By that time both Karen and Brannigan had come to his side. "I'm all right," he told the girl quickly, noting the anxiety in her glance. It sent a tingle through his aching body to see her frank concern but his next words were for Brannigan. "Fur thieves robbed the freight wagon for Sheridan yesterday morning, Lieutenant," he said. "They stole every pelt and killed both teamsters. We took the trail at dawn today. We tracked them up the valley to the little brook just below here. There they split into two parties. Two of them came this way and the other two took the pack horses and rode out into the creek. Coulter and Yerg are following that trail now."

"Sit down, men!" Brannigan's voice was sharp as he saw the condition of the other two. "How long have you fellows been riding?"

"About sixteen hours, sir," Barstow replied.

"With Shelby just out of the hospital! Who was crazy enough to let him do a thing like that?"

Speers let a flicker of a grin slide across his unshaven lips. "Major O'Rourke, sir."

Brannigan turned abruptly to Shelby, hiding his embarrassment by asking another question. "Do you know the identity of the thieves?"

"We've got a pretty good hunch. If we guessed right you had a couple of visitors this morning. One of them was either Hogan or Pew."

198

The lieutenant stared. "We had both of them in here just after breakfast. They claimed they had ridden up White Water Valley scouting for Bonsall's surveying crew. They stopped here for about fifteen minutes and then rode on toward the pass that leads across to the Moccasin."

A hail from the brush distracted the attention of the little group and they turned to see Coulter and Yerg riding in from the direction of the creek. Shelby hesitated a moment before commenting on Brannigan's information. Then he said:

"I reckon they stopped here just long enough to keep the men interested while the other two bandits circled the camp with the pelts. See if Coulter and Yerg don't check me on that."

Brannigan waited silently until the two troopers rode up and dismounted. Coulter made a determined effort at a smart salute, reporting directly to the officer but obviously intending his words for Shelby. "Reporting in from detail, sir. Trail of the bandits runs up the valley on the other side o' the crick. Two men each leadin' two horses."

Brannigan swung on Sergeant Andrews. "Sergeant, you're our best tracker. Take three men and investigate that trail. Try to find out if Hogan and Pew joined the others above the camp. See if they went on toward Moccasin Valley."

The realization that someone was taking over the responsibility completed the letdown for Tom. He could surrender to his weariness now; no longer did he have to force himself ahead. He knew that Karen had

199

stooped to slip a supporting arm around his shoulders and he certainly wasn't in any hurry to change that!

Brannigan's orders flew sharply and through the haze of fatigue which had enveloped him Shelby caught a phrase here and there. The detachment was getting ready for action.

He managed a final spurt of energy when he realized that men were helping him to his feet. They were taking him to that generous log house which had been constructed on the site of the destroyed cabin. Then someone handed him a tin cup full of scalding coffee and the bitterness of the strong brew revived him a little.

The troopers had deposited him on a bunk, Karen and Brannigan standing nearby. He managed a rueful grin. "This must get monotonous for you folks," he said. "You're always doing all the work while I lie around and have somebody wait on me. If I don't stay on my feet better than this I'll be taking root."

"Sixteen hours in the saddle when you're still a hospital case!" Brannigan snapped. "Any more stunts like that and you'll know all about roots — from the wrong end. Now take it easy and give me the whole story. I want to know what we're up against."

Shelby told him, mentioning the fight at the stage station because it explained the expulsion of the Bonsall gang from Fort Butler. It never occurred to him that he was offering no explanation for his own presence in Nan Elson's home. He saw the odd look Brannigan turned on Karen but he couldn't understand the strange mixture of emotions which seemed to be in

200

it. Brannigan seemed to be saying, "I told you so." It didn't make sense.

When he had completed his story Brannigan nodded grimly. "So it's killers and road agents we have to deal with now! That means we'll have to take the trail at once. The men are well rested and a night march won't hurt them."

"Better not go tonight," Tom counseled. "I've got a notion Bonsall isn't in on this fur robbery. Hogan's crowd will probably cache the pelts before they get back to the main camp, figuring to let things cool off a bit before they try to market their loot. If you ride tonight you'll miss any sign of where they might leave the trail to make their cache."

Brannigan considered for some moments before he nodded thoughtfully. "That sounds possible — but what makes you think Bonsall isn't a party to the theft? I wouldn't put anything past that bird!"

"Just a hunch, I reckon. He's mean enough for most anything, but this business of outright highway robbery is a little out of his line. He has to have some crooked law on his side when he makes a move — as well as some kind of salve for his warped conscience. Remember the way he cussed me for a Rebel when he was trying to find an excuse to ride out into the Moccasin? That's the pattern of both his craziness and his crookedness. He's not in on the robbery."

Karen had waited silently since entering the cabin. At first she had listened to Tom's story but at the reference to the stage station fight she turned abruptly to the work of tending her evening meal. Supper had been nearly ready when the interruption occurred so it didn't take her long to produce a steaming bowl of stew. She brought it to the bunk, her smile not quite convincing as she pulled out a stool and sat down beside Shelby. "Look alive, invalid," she said, trying to sound casually jolly. "Get ready to be fed. I'm not used to this spoon feeding so don't complain if I pour some of it down your neck."

Brannigan watched silently for a moment. Then he moved toward the door. "I'll check up on Andrews," he said shortly.

He left a strained silence behind him. Karen's opening attempt at levity had not fooled either of them. Something had come between them and Tom could not be sure what it was. He wondered if perhaps she was trying to find a way to tell him what he had been fearing all along.

"I suppose you know we're broke," he said abruptly. "Loss of those pelts means I can't meet the cattle payment."

"I understand," she replied. "My luck hasn't been any better. There was no trace of the diamonds in Moccasin Valley and they were certainly not here in the ashes of the house. I suppose we should get word to that cattleman who is to bring the herd. Perhaps he can divert the drive to some other market."

"We might — if you know who he is and where he is coming from."

"I don't. It was my father's deal, you know."

"Well, there's no use worrying yet. The boys may be able to recover the pelts. Then we can go through with it."

She eyed him seriously. "Are you sure you still want to go through with it? After all, you have no obligation to use your money that way. You can buy the number of cows you need for your own use — and use them to suit yourself. The rest of the problem is my worry. You don't have to shoulder it."

"You sound like you're proposing that we give up the partnership idea." He tried to keep his voice calm but it wasn't a very good try. Finally the axe had fallen. She was trying to tell him that she had changed her mind about him. Brannigan had made good use of his time.

"I'm not proposing it," she replied. "It was your idea in the first place and it was your money that was to carry it out. I just don't want to tie you down to a deal which would be unfair to you — particularly when it seems we made a mistake in our choice of partners."

There it was! He wished she could have been more direct and have used less of that talk about being unfair to him. He would have preferred to remember her as she had been before, frank and open, telling him that it was Dan Brannigan and not Tom Shelby. This way it sounded a little cheap.

He had to swallow hard before he could control himself enough to say, "If that's the way you want it." Then he turned his face to the wall.

He could hear her moving slowly across to the fireplace, then Brannigan's voice boomed from the doorway. "Looks like you figured it right, Shelby.

203

Sergeant Andrews says the two men with their four pack horses joined Hogan and Pew at the mouth of the pass. They went on across toward the Moccasin. We'll take the trail at dawn."

Tom crawled out from under the blanket which covered him. Every movement was agony now that his muscles had been given a chance to stiffen but he was determined to leave the cabin. "I'm going along," he said thickly. "I'll bunk outside with you and be ready."

"Easy there," Brannigan warned, taking a step forward. "Get back in that bunk and rest."

As he caught Tom's arm he could see the flush which had crept into the weary man's cheeks. Immediately his tone became more stern. "Man, you've got a fever! Get into that bunk and stay there. I'll have a soldier come in to help Miss Neilson."

Shelby tried to protest but already his effort had made him dizzy. It was easier to do as he was told. Anyway, he had no inclination to argue about anything. The bubble had burst. Why bother?

The mental letdown had its prompt physical effect. Even before a man could be detailed to orderly duties Shelby had dropped off into an exhausted slumber.

At first there was the complete unconsciousness of deep sleep, then fitful dreams began to trouble him. Two or three times it seemed almost as though he were awake, his pain soothed by the calming touch of Karen Neilson's fingers on his brow and temples. Always it was completely dark and his weary brain could never piece things out before sleep would drug him once more.

204

Finally he awoke to find a faint rectangle of gray heralding a dawn beyond the doorway. A stir of men and animals mingled with the creak and clatter of equipment. The detachment was preparing to ride out on the trail of the fur thieves.

There was no sign of Karen but presently he became aware of regular breathing close at hand. For a moment he couldn't locate the sound but then he realized that she was stretched out on the floor beside the bunk, sound asleep. Maybe those dreams hadn't been all dreams after all. He felt a twinge of conscience that he had used her bunk while she slept on the floor but there was no time for him to fret over that. The dark bulk of a man appeared in the doorway and Brannigan's voice came softly. "Karen. Are you awake?"

Tom could have strangled him cheerfully for the way he spoke the name but instead he remained silent. If Brannigan had come to take leave of the girl it would be the part of decency to let them alone. Whether Brannigan had played fair or not was of no moment now. Karen had made her choice and she deserved a chance for happiness.

He kept his eyes shut tightly, listening to the sounds of her stealthy movements. She was trying not to disturb him and he appreciated her thoughtfulness even as he cursed his luck at losing her.

It surprised him a little when he heard them go out into the morning twilight. They had halted just beyond the doorway and were conversing in low tones. He tried to make himself listen to the sounds of the camp but the voices at the door meant too much to him to make that possible.

He gave them a reasonable time to themselves, then he swung aching legs to the floor and struggled across to the doorway. "Sorry to interrupt, folks," he said cheerfully — "but I want to see the parade. Best of luck and all that."

"You get back to bed!" Brannigan grinned. "I'm leaving Karen in command of a squad. She'll have the men sit on you if you don't behave."

Shelby could have kicked him. What right did the big galoot have to be so happy?

Because he thought he knew the answer to that he went back to the bunk and stretched himself out again. One thing about it, after this experience with people he would certainly have sense enough to stay out in the hills by himself!

CHAPTER
TWENTY-ONE

Karen didn't come back into the cabin until the camp was quiet again. Tom could imagine her standing out there gazing after Brannigan and the thought woke a fierce anger in him. It was going to be difficult to keep up this pretense of being generous. A man didn't pass up a girl like Karen without showing the effects.

When she entered, her eyes met his briefly but beyond a bare greeting at seeing him awake she kept silent. He watched her as she went about her breakfast work, trying to determine the meaning of this strained silence. Finally, he could stand it no longer. Kicking off the blanket he sat up on the edge of the bunk, trying to make his head stop whirling. "I'm getting out of here," he said flatly. "This invalid business is getting in my hair!"

That wasn't the point of the matter but Karen didn't bother to call him on it. Instead she simply walked to the door and called, "Hey, Jeff! Bring your gang; the patient is getting delirious."

Her grin when she turned back into the room was the first smile he had seen from her since the previous evening. The corners of his mouth quirked in response. "You're a hard gal to beat," he complained. "That's what makes me feel so bad about losing you. If you'd just be stupid or dull once in a while maybe I could get over it."

She frowned quickly, uncertain as to his mood. So much of the time he was joking she never could depend too much on his seriousness. Finally she decided to play it his way. "Go ahead and suffer," she said coolly. "It was your choice. I hope your regrets haunt you to an early grave."

It was his turn to stare but the entrance of Speers gave him no chance to pursue the matter. Jeff was in fine fettle after a night's rest and his first glance told him that Karen's hail had been largely a threat rather than a true call for help. He waved back the trooper who had accompanied him. "Won't need you, Sam. Me and a cordwood stick can handle one invalid, I reckon."

The spinning had stopped in Shelby's head now. He met Jeff's salute with a sly grin. "Talking big, hey?" he jeered. "Save your strutting 'til you get back to Nan. You'll need your nerve and your cordwood sticks when you start tryin' to hold your own with a woman who's so handy at slinging chairs."

He caught Karen's puzzled look and explained. "Since you left the fort Jeff has gone romantic on us. He found a soft spot in Nan Elson's otherwise sensible nature and persuaded her to marry him. Maybe I wasn't modest enough to mention it but Jeff had a small part in the stage station fight. He sat on the floor and groaned while Mrs. Elson and I fought fourteen bandits. I figure that's when the tender passion really blossomed. Nan felt sorry for the poor ugly cuss and agreed to take care of him."

Jeff was enjoying the recital, confident that Karen would understand. "Every feller to his own taste," he drawled. "It ain't my fault if Tommy likes to train with bandits while I pick better-lookin' company."

Karen wasn't paying any attention to the nonsense now. At Shelby's story she had stepped forward, a sudden tense expression killing her smile of amusement. "You mean Jeff is going to marry Nan Elson?" she demanded.

"Sure." Tom was still forcing his humor to keep his own mind from his troubles. "Maybe I didn't make myself clear on that but it's sure enough the main point of the yarn. Of course, he's nowhere near good enough for her but then who would he be good enough for? . . . For that matter, I can't see how any confounded lieutenant is good enough for . . . All right, I won't say it."

There was something almost like a smile on her lips as she turned her back on him. Maybe the smile was for Jeff. At least her words were. "Congratulations," she said. "I'm sure you'll both be very happy."

He took the outstretched hand, his own grin wide. "Thanks. Maybe one o' these days I can say the same for you."

Her smile had broadened but she kept her back on Shelby as she replied. "No prospects, I'm afraid. Tom and I have agreed to disagree. I thought he was falling in love with Nan and he keeps deluding himself into the ridiculous belief that I have lost my heart to Lieutenant

Brannigan. Of course, both ideas are ridiculous but there's not much use of us trying to get along when we insist on misunderstanding each other like that."

Shelby's whistle was long-drawn-out, the rising pitch at the end indicating his dawning comprehension. "Will you run that speech over again?" he asked slowly. "I want to know whether I'm out of my head or whether a ray of light is just beginning to seep through my thick skull. Haven't you been trying to give me the gate with all this talk about wrong partners?"

Karen still didn't turn to face him. She simply took Jeff's elbow and steered him toward the door. "Bless your heart and get out of here," she said softly. "A couple of idiots need a little time to get caught up with themselves."

Jeff obeyed, turning briefly at the door to give a very good imitation of Shelby's voice. "Ah, Spring!" he quoted. "What it won't do to young critters!"

Then he was gone and Karen was facing Tom, a tremulous smile on her lips. "Whatever made you think I wanted Dan Brannigan, you goose?"

He kept his smile, using it now to cover a new lot of emotions. "I figured maybe he had money enough to buy cows for you. Of course, he ain't as pretty as me but a good business woman like you wouldn't think of things like . . ."

It would have been foolish to continue such a sentence. Besides, her hair was tickling his nose. She laughed happily in his arms. "What a silly pair we have been!" she exclaimed after a moment or two. "I really don't know which one of us was worse."

210

"Let's not start an argument about that," he chuckled. "I'll compromise on any terms you offer."

She kissed him suddenly and wriggled out of his arms. "I'll bet I've hurt your sore ribs," she said, very penitent. "I completely forgot about them when I flung myself at you."

"So did I," he told her. "Anyway I'm still so numb with the surprise of it all that I can't even feel sore spots."

To prove his boast he tried to stand erect. Karen sprang forward as he grunted and sank back. "Lie down!" she ordered briskly. "You've got to take care of yourself so I can put you to work. Maybe you don't remember but we're bankrupt and in a pretty mess."

"What mess?" he scoffed, easing himself into a comfortable position. "Now that I know you're not losing your head over a uniform I haven't a worry in the world. What's a little thing like pelts or cattle or diamonds? I don't have a care!"

She moved over to sit beside him, more carefully now but with just as complete satisfaction to both of them.

It seemed like all of ten minutes later that Sergeant Andrews and six troopers rode into the clearing. Actually it was late afternoon but the passage of time had been a matter of little concern to Tom and Karen. The rest and the sudden turn of fortune had done wonders for Shelby. He was still hobbling around stiffly but there was none of the threatened fever which had concerned Karen last night.

They were sitting together in the cabin doorway when the men came out of the timber. Tom could see that none of the troopers looked very happy but he couldn't quite understand the disgusted look on Andrews' grizzled countenance.

"What luck, Sarge?" he asked when the non-com stopped before them.

"No luck at all. We went through the pass at an easy pace, watchin' fer sign all the way. The trail was easy to follow and I'd swear they never went off on either side. Howsomever, when we run across them in the Moccasin they seemed plumb innocent. They was all in camp together, Bonsall, Hogan, Pew, the five new men and a messenger from Major O'Rourke. There wasn't a pelt around and no sign of 'em havin' hid anything anywhere."

"What kind of a yarn did they tell?"

"Smooth enough one. Old Bonsall was mighty sharp with 'em and it looks to me like they ain't jest seein' eye to eye over there. It didn't shake Hogan's story, though. He claimed the four of 'em rode up this valley fer a quick look at the country. Him and Pew covered this side of the flat while Daniels and the Swede took the other side."

"What did Lieutenant Brannigan say to that?"

"Not much. It had us all puzzled. Both Bonsall and the trooper who had camped with 'em overnight swore there hadn't been any pelts brought into the valley. We knew they didn't cache any between here and there. It makes it look like you boys slipped up on your trackin'. Anybody as dog tired as you was last night coulda mixed trails easy. Somewhere down the valley you lost the sign of the fur bandits and picked up the trail of Hogan and his pals."

Coulter and Speers had come up to listen. It was Coulter who entered an angry denial. "None of us was *that* tired, Sarge! Hogan's gang stole the pelts, all right. You boys jest let Bonsall pull the wool over your eyes!"

Andrews tugged uneasily at his straggly mustache. "You can argue that out with the lieutenant," he said shortly. "I'm just tellin' you what I saw and what he told me to tell you."

Shelby had come down out of the clouds with a jolt. He had expected trouble but a mystery like this was something he hadn't bargained for. Andrews was a competent tracker and a pretty levelheaded sort of a man. He would not have been fooled by a clever hiding job or by a smooth yarn. Something was plenty wrong somewhere.

"What happened to the others?" he asked Andrews.

"They're headin' down the Moccasin. Somethin' is up at the fort and the major sent for us. The lieutenant kept on down the valley and sent us back to tell you the yarn and pick up these other bummers. We'll hit the trail in the mornin'. He said to send you both his best regards."

Jeff let out a sudden yelp of excitement but covered it with an elaborate yawn. Stretching mightily he drawled, "Well, as long as you boys are stuck and I can't hang around here much longer to take care o' things, I reckon I'd better give you a hint."

Tom watched him narrowly. For all his act it was obvious that Speers was excited about something. The lanky fellow waited for his remark to have its proper effect, then he went on, "Maybe you remember I wanted to search a certain little brook below here? The sign was all mixed up and it looked like the polecats was havin' a confab. Well, right there is where they ducked offa the trail to hide their loot, not takin' a chance on runnin' it by the camp. Daniels and the squarehead jest circled the clearin' to keep the extra horses out o' sight. Any of you greenhorns want to go help a good man find some pelts?"

It didn't take long for the whole crowd of troopers to be on their way down the valley. Temporarily free from real discipline they entered into the hunt with all the excitement of kids on a paper chase. Jeff rode in the lead with Karen, explaining loftily why he hadn't stated his theory before.

Tom stayed behind alone, very much against his will. He had argued until Karen took a hand in the conversation, then he subsided. After all, he wasn't anxious to get into a saddle again just yet. Karen could make certain that no part of the glen was missed.

Dusk had begun to drop its smoky mantle over the valley when the little cavalcade reappeared among the trees. Jeff no longer led the way and Tom could read failure in his crestfallen appearance. The pelts had not been found.

"I just figgered wrong, that's all," Jeff growled. "They never went up that brook at all."

214

"And they didn't stop anywhere along the crick," Yerg put in. "Coulter and me can swear to that."

Andrews yanked at his mustache again. "Mebbe the lieutenant was right," he suggested. "You boys musta missed your sign somewhere down the valley. We'll watch sharp when we ride down that way come mornin'. Furs don't dry up and blow away."

It was a silent camp that evening, the element of mystery keeping everybody occupied with much the same thoughts. Tom, Jeff and Karen spent the time together in the cabin, going over every step of the chase and trying to think of a spot where they might have missed anything. It wasn't until Jeff rose to go that there was a break in the thought.

Then Tom straightened up carefully and went over to get the blanket he had carried behind his saddle. "I'll sleep outside," he said shortly.

She looked up questioningly but without saying anything. Tom went on, floundering a little as he tried to sound casual. "I'm well enough so that I don't have to be babied any more — and I'm not well enough to stand the strain of having you around all the time."

She blushed, giving him a quick glance from beneath lowered lashes. "Maybe you're right," she retorted. "When you talk like that you're not safe to have around."

Andrews and the troopers hit the trail soon after sun-up. It was a fine morning and the men were in good spirits, joking broadly about leaving Tom and

215

Karen alone. Tom tried to turn the banter on Jeff, apparently not seriously concerned about it, but when the troopers had disappeared into the timber he turned a troubled face to Karen.

"We'll have to do something about this," he told her. "With all the partnership talk and so many troubles cropping up I clean forgot about the way folks gossip. I reckon we'd better take a trip in to Fort Butler. There's a chaplain there and anyway I need to bring out the supplies I bought."

She smiled with frank amusement. "That wouldn't be your idea of a romantic proposal, would it?" she asked. "Or have you forgotten that you never did attend to that little detail?"

He stammered for a moment, then laughed aloud. "I was waiting for you to do it," he told her. "Everything else has worked backward for us. You bossed the house building. You had first claim on the land. I was the one who was carried over the threshold — even if you didn't do the carrying. I'm feeling more like a bride all the time."

"Stop dodging the question!" she scolded. "Are you going to propose decently or not?"

He grabbed her by the shoulders and held her close. His head came down until the tip of his nose was almost touching hers. Then, glaring melodramatically, he growled, "Let's you and me git hitched, gal."

"I give up," she laughed — and kissed him. "I'll never get anything really romantic out of you. You're just the chore man and I'm the cook, I'm afraid."

216

After that they didn't talk very much for some time. Finally he released her and she stepped back a pace, smoothing down her disordered hair. "You're entirely too rough to be rated on sick call any more," she laughed. "How are you at chopping wood?"

"I'm better at this," he retorted. "Come back here."

The scene froze as two quick shots sounded on the morning air. They were distant and for a moment Tom wondered if Andrews had run into some kind of an ambush. Maybe the Indians had come back into the valley.

Then a third shot — and a fourth — came to give him a bearing. This time he knew that the shooting was somewhere back in the pass.

"Here we go!" he said grimly. "Get your rifle and we'll bar the door. Any visitors from Moccasin Valley are a bad risk."

CHAPTER
TWENTY-TWO

Shelby had not appreciated the really fine work the soldiers had done in constructing the cabin. Now he saw many good points as he set about preparing for defense. Heavy shutters had been provided for the windows, a loophole in each shutter at the lower left hand corner so that a defender's body would be protected by the heavy log wall.

"Smart arrangement," he commented quietly. "Whose idea was this? Yours or Brannigan's?"

Karen locked a shutter into place and ran quickly to another window. "Sergeant Andrews was construction boss. He must have been the one who planned the shutters."

"Good man. I wish we had him here now — with about a dozen of Brannigan's boys."

Wishing didn't stop his activity. Once the shutters were in place he turned to other preparations, seeing to the placing of ammunition and the proper loading of their three weapons. The water bucket was full and there was a good supply of food in the house. Unless an unexpectedly strong enemy should attack they could withstand quite a siege.

"Keep moving from one loophole to another," he directed. "I'll stay here where I can keep an eye on the corral. If it's Indians we have to reckon with their first move will be aimed at the horses."

"You think it's Indians?" she queried, her voice steady.

"May be. Driving Indians away doesn't mean a thing. They keep coming back if they like the country."

"But I thought you were chiefly concerned about what Captain Bonsall might do."

"I was — but they wouldn't advertise their coming by doing all of that shooting. It's just possible that they were heading this way and ran afoul of an Indian scouting party. We'll have to look out for almost anything until we learn what that shooting meant."

The minutes dragged along without further conversation interfering with vigilance. Then Shelby broke the silence with a mirthless chuckle. "And I was bothered by thoughts of gossip!" he exclaimed. "We're here alone, all right. I wonder what the scandalmongers would think of this?"

"It never worried me," she laughed — "but I wouldn't mind a few chaperones just now. Blue-coated ones with guns."

"Can't look for that, I'm afraid. The army has done more than its bit for us. From here in it's our fight — and I'm glad of it. I was getting pretty weary of having other people wait on me all the time . . ."

"It's our fight," she repeated. "And we'll make it a good one. The stakes are worth while."

He grinned without taking his eyes from the scene at the corral. "Meaning me, of course?" he asked.

"Meaning the land," she corrected. "I already have you — whatever good you are. Now we're fighting for this *free* land. I wonder what it will cost us this time?"

He remembered an earlier comment like that. One of them — he couldn't remember which — had said that the land was not free; it had to be paid for in hardship and suffering rather than in dollars. It pleased him that he couldn't remember who had made the remark, that their thoughts were so alike as to be indistinguishable.

An hour dragged by with no change in the situation except that the cabin was becoming quite warm. Outside the valley seemed peaceful and Tom began to grow restless.

"See any crows?" he asked abruptly.

"A few. Why?"

"I'll trade windows with you for a while. I want to see how the birds are acting up the valley."

They traded places and Shelby spent some minutes in a careful study of the upper valley. Finally he spoke again. "I'm going on a scout. The crows are flapping around in the greatest of peace. They wouldn't be doing that if there were men in the timber. Bar the door after me and keep a close lookout. We can't stay cooped up like this without knowing what it's all about."

She reached for her hat. "If you think I'm staying here you're crazy! I'm going with you."

"But that's a useless risk. You can't . . ."

"Yes, I can — whatever it is. I'd rather take my chances out there with you than to stay here alone and wonder what was happening. Anyway, you're not fit to ride alone. Nurse goes along!"

Her voice was almost bantering but there was determination in the corners of her mouth. "Fair enough — partner," he agreed. "Keep me covered while I go for the horses. There's just a chance of Indians lurking out there in the trees. Shoot if you see anything move."

She nodded and went back to the loophole which he had guarded so long. Tom went out quickly, every nerve alert as he crossed to the corral and roped Useless and the pinto. Nothing came to interrupt him, however, and he was back at the cabin without delay. Karen met him at the door, lugging a saddle rig. "I'll ride the paint horse," she announced firmly. "It's time I got acquainted with him and let you ride your own old bag of bones."

"Meaning you're afraid the pinto will be too rough for my sore ribs," he retorted. "All right, I won't argue. I'd lose — and besides I think it's time I stopped you from getting too thick with Useless. Look at him now! Ignoring me and trying to take a friendly bite out of you!"

It relieved the tension to joke thus as they left the clearing but it didn't take Shelby's attention from the task at hand. At any other time it would have been mighty pleasant to ride up the sunny valley with such a girl but now his thoughts were divided elsewhere. He was watching the ground for sign and at the same time keeping careful tab on the birds. So long as crows kept flying up at their approach he felt certain that no enemies lurked in ambush.

They entered the pass and their vigilance redoubled. Regardless of the peacefulness of the birds someone had done some shooting in here not very long ago. That someone might still be here, waiting for new targets.

Karen hadn't said a word since leaving the clearing but she wasn't missing anything. She rode easily, her rifle cradled in the crook of her arm and her alert glance scanning the woodland on either side.

They climbed the gentle slope of the lower pass and were just entering a narrow defile when Shelby pulled up abruptly and clambered from the saddle. "Stay close to the trees and keep your eyes open," he said softly. "Here's where it happened."

He studied the sign for several minutes, then led Useless forward, motioning for Karen to follow. A hundred yards up the pass he stopped again, once more scrutinizing the sign which Karen couldn't even see. Finally he turned with a puzzled frown. "Looks like two men were overtaken and shot by two others. Then the killers loaded the bodies — or the wounded men — on their horses and went back toward Moccasin Valley. All four horses were shod — and at least one seems mighty familiar."

He moved forward again, trying to puzzle the thing out. Open war must have broken out in Bonsall's camp. The queer part was that he would have expected Bonsall and Dombrek to be the refugees — but it looked to be the big bay of Daniels which had been riding in the lead.

222

The trail became rocky, a mere ledge along the side of the gulch. Occupied with the task of reading sign on the bare rocks Tom might have missed the startling discovery if Karen hadn't spotted a flash of color below.

At her sharp exclamation Tom looked up, then peered down into the ravine where she was pointing. There were two bodies down there, partly hidden by brush but with plenty of sign to tell the story.

"Pursuers caught them back there and shot them," he remarked slowly. "Then they brought the bodies this far before dumping them into the gulch. Watch sharp now and I'll have a look."

It was tedious work getting his aching muscles down the rocky declivity but soon he stood beside the battered corpses of Daniels and Svenson. Both men had wounds in their backs while Daniels had been shot again in the chest. A quick search of their clothing revealed nothing more and Tom climbed back to the trail, pausing only to start a shale slide which would bury the dead men.

"Find me an answer to that one!" he challenged Karen when he had recovered his wind. "I figured Bonsall and Dombrek had been caught in a rebellion but it's a couple of our fur-stealing friends."

"Maybe Bonsall had them killed to protect himself."

He shrugged. "I pass. What we need around here is a gypsy fortune teller. Nothing makes sense."

They rode back in thoughtful silence. Neither spoke until they were in the clearing before the corral. Then Tom remarked, "I wish I'd thought to ask Andrews about the location of Bonsall's camp. If this business gets any thicker it might be well to know the location of the enemy."

"Maybe I can help," Karen suggested. "I came through Moccasin Valley, you know, and I don't believe there is a decent camping place above the scene of the battle. The valley was pretty badly burned."

He nodded absently and she went on, trying to give him the picture. "There was a camp site where we stopped. It was in the little strip of clear valley between the Indian village and the battlefield. I suspect Bonsall might have camped there."

Shelby had slid from the saddle before her words struck home. Then he looked up with a quick grunt. "Little strip?" he echoed. "How far was the village from the scene of the fight?"

She stared. "Weren't you there?"

"Part way. I stopped and went to sleep before I ever reached the Indian camp."

"I forgot. I don't think it could have been more than three hundred yards. Just a strip of woodland in between."

He grabbed her and kissed her enthusiastically as she swung to the ground beside him. "Why didn't somebody tell me that before?" he exclaimed. "Why didn't I think of it? I might have known those superstitious heathens would have moved!"

His excitement was obvious as he hugged her tightly. "A brain storm at last! I'm going to Moccasin Valley, my beauteous damsel — and you're staying here! Don't give me any arguments this time. I know where the diamonds are!"

224

He stripped the saddle from the pinto and turned the pony loose in the corral, ignoring Karen's volley of questions. It wasn't until they turned back toward the cabin, with Tom still leading Useless, that he gave her any kind of a hint. Then he spoke to the roan. "We're going places, boy," he confided. "Shall we let her in on the secret?"

The horse tossed his head a couple of times and Tom laughed aloud. "So she's got you on a string too, has she? I reckon I'll have to tell her."

He left Useless standing at the door and led the way into the cabin. Then with his finger he scratched a rude map on the dirt floor. "This is Moccasin Valley," he explained. "Here at the head of the valley is the opening where the pass comes out. About three miles down the creek is where we fought the Indians." He marked both spots. "Now show me the location of the Indian camp where Bonsall did his famous digging act."

She scratched a mark directly beside the place where he had indicated the battle.

"Good," he approved. "The village I watched was a good two miles up the valley, only about a mile below the pass. Bonsall tore up the wrong place."

"You mean there were two villages?"

"No. Just one — but there were two locations for it. Indians are superstitious devils. They won't stay in a spot which they think is bad medicine any more than they'll take the warpath when the signs are wrong. Lightning struck their village just when they were making war medicine. That was a bad omen so they naturally moved out. I should have thought of that before. Bonsall searched the place where he found them, not the place where they had been when your mother was taken captive. I suppose the fire destroyed all traces of the old site and of the moving."

"And you think the diamonds are where my mother buried them?"

"I'd bet on it! I'm leaving for the Moccasin just as soon as I can get ready. It'll give me daylight for most of the journey and I can search the right village at dawn. That way I should be able to avoid Bonsall's crowd."

"But won't you be likely to run into them in the pass? If two of his men were killed there they must be using that part of the hills for some purpose."

"I doubt it. Right now the only thing I can see about that killing is the fact that we have two less bad hombres to worry about. Now stop the argument and get some grub together. I thought your part of this deal was to be the cook."

She pulled a rueful grin. "You certainly are trying to keep me domestic! Why shouldn't I go along on this trip? I didn't cause you any trouble before."

He pulled her to him exuberantly. "You're a swell partner," he told her, "but this time it's better to play it my way. If anything should happen to me you still have a chance of getting down the valley for help. After that you can follow up the hint I just gave you. On the other hand, if I run into trouble and have to ride for it, I'll be mighty glad to have reserves to fall back on. You'll be more useful here."

She saluted. "Very good, General. The reserves will be ready. Try not to need them."

CHAPTER
TWENTY-THREE

Night had fallen when Shelby emerged from the pass and started down Moccasin Valley. Even in the darkness he could sense familiar country, the pine-clad slopes rising black on either side. Apparently the fire had not swept this far up the Moccasin.

The ride from the White Water had scarcely been kind to his aching body but this time he did not feel that sickening exhaustion which had gripped him two days before. He was getting back into condition, only a bad case of stiff muscles remaining to recall his sojourn in the hospital.

He moved with extreme care as he worked his way downstream. There was little chance of finding Bonsall camped so far toward the head of the valley but he still wasn't taking any unnecessary chances. It wouldn't do to blunder into them in the dark or to give them any hint of his presence.

Within a half mile of the pass he began to smell the tang of burned wood. He was entering the belt of the forest fire and it gave him a quick feeling of satisfaction. So far his hunch was proving correct; Bear Nose's old village site had burned over, thus concealing the fact that the camp had been moved.

It was aggravating to have to continue past the clearing where he had watched the war dance. Right there within a few yards of him was probably the Neilson diamonds but he knew it would be useless to search for them in the darkness. Moreover, he wanted a look at Bonsall's camp. Coming through the pass he had thought of a startling possibility and he was anxious to see whether Hogan and Pew were still with the land grabber crew.

Rounding a bend in the valley he could see the gleam of a fire in the distance. It was over a mile away, he calculated, but he wasn't anxious to ride nearer. He ranged closer to the creek and presently found a clump of bushes which the fire had missed, probably because the flood waters had been over the lower flats at that time. He picketed Useless with his customary low-toned admonitions and struck out down the valley afoot.

It required the better part of an hour for him to work his way into a position which commanded the camp, but the scene was worth the effort. Without doubt there was trouble in the ranks of the surveying crew. Either a break had already occurred or one was very near. Bonsall and Dombrek sat together in the shadows, silent for the most part and never taking their eyes from the five desperadoes who sat at the other side of the fire. All seven of them wore their weapons and the obvious tension in the camp told why.

Tom couldn't hear any of the talk although once in a while a raucous voice boomed out as a burly blackbeard resorted to profane bravado. Tom recalled seeing him at Fort Butler, a powerful brute of a man whose greasy clothing shone villainously in the firelight.

The other two were equally nameless to Shelby but he studied them carefully. One was tall, lanky and completely bald. Tom recalled vaguely that the man was grotesquely cross-eyed but he couldn't verify the memory at that distance. The other fellow was short and dumpy, a rotund man of middle age whose red whiskers were as unkempt as the black ones of the loud man.

It wasn't a pleasant-looking crowd to reckon with but Tom felt satisfied as he backed cautiously away. Hogan and Pew were still in the valley — and there was a good chance of civil war in the enemy's ranks. A man couldn't hope for much more than that.

He found Useless without difficulty. "Here we go again, hoss," he announced cheerfully. "We'll see if we can't find another unburned spot somewhere above the bend. I don't want to be in sight of that camp when daylight comes."

He was lucky enough to find another green clump in the sea of charred vegetation, this one at the very edge of the Indian camp site. There he rolled himself in his blanket and was almost immediately asleep.

A murky dawn was upon the valley when he awoke. New aches stabbed at his back and legs but he wasn't letting mere stiff muscles bother him now. There was a job to be done, a job which should be completed before anyone from Bonsall's camp could start snooping.

He moved Useless hastily across the old village site, picketing the roan in the bushes above the clearing.

Then taking a spade-bayonet from his blanket roll he went back to hunt for the spot where he had lain that night of the storm.

The fire had changed the appearance of the place but presently he felt fairly certain of his position. Directly across from him the rock wall rose abruptly, a shattered pine black against the gray stone. In line with that tree and almost at its base would be the spot where the tepee had stood. He was about to sight from another direction but his searching glance caught the blackened embers there. Fragments of the blasted tepee still remained to mark the precise spot!

Sure of himself now he hurried across. The Indians had disposed of Mrs. Neilson's body but they had not cleared away the rubble when they moved out. He hesitated briefly, then set to work at the edge of the circle nearest the creek. That would be the side farthest from the doorway, the side Mrs. Neilson would probably have used in concealing her precious package from the fiends.

He turned over the ground carefully, working only to a depth of about eight inches. It was not likely that the unfortunate woman would have ventured to dig a deeper hole than that, particularly if she had been handicapped for lack of digging tools.

He had been working nearly fifteen minutes when the dull point of the bayonet struck something soft yet unyielding. He dropped the tool quickly and dug down into the moist soil with his fingers, uncovering a small chamois bag which had been rolled and tied with a piece of tape. Its contents shifted under the pressure of

230

his fingers and he knew that he was holding a small fortune in gems, a fortune which had already been the indirect cause of several deaths. Certainly the troopers who had died in the Indian fight would not have met their fate if Bonsall had not been obsessed with a desire to obtain this bag which he didn't really appreciate for its true value.

Tom straightened up, stretching a kink out of his back as he shoved the bag into a pants pocket. Then he squatted awkwardly to pick up the spade-bayonet. The move saved his life for as he went down a slug whined just above his head and a rifle cracked viciously from down the valley.

He came up running, shifting the bayonet to his left hand and reaching for his .44. The rifle barked again and this time Shelby saw the puff of smoke. Someone was sniping at him from the belt of timber below the clearing.

Running low and zig-zagging, he headed for the spot where he had left the roan. Another glance over his shoulder showed him two riders breaking out of the woods and galloping toward him. Both carried rifles so he didn't stop to argue the matter with his six-gun. A smart man didn't give away that kind of odds!

They had closed the gap appreciably by the time he reached his horse but now he didn't feel so badly about it. He yanked the Spencer from its boot and raced across to a blackened tree where he wouldn't be putting Useless in the line of fire.

The two riders were close now and one of them snapped a shot as he saw Tom dive for cover. It was the loud-mouthed bandit with the black whiskers. Shelby held the Spencer's front sight on the lower fringe of black beard and pulled the trigger gently.

The other man wheeled his horse as his companion went down, triggering one wild shot before fleeing in sudden panic. Shelby let him go. It was foolish, he knew, but he couldn't bring himself to shoot even a rogue in the back.

He kept the Spencer in his hand as he untied Useless and mounted. Behind him he could hear Hogan's angry bellow. That meant the fight would be renewed. There would be a chase when the surviving bushwhacker told his story. Even Bonsall might join with the others when he learned that Tom Shelby was now in possession of the long-sought bag.

It was hard to keep from forcing the pace as he sent Useless up the grade into the pass but Tom realized that he was in no shape for a long, hard ride. Until the emergency came he would have to save himself, hoping there would be something left when showdown time arrived.

Useless maintained a steady pace and when they reached the crest of the little divide Tom was almost ready to believe that there was to be no immediate pursuit. It was a sight of the gulch which hid the bodies of Daniels and Svenson which brought back his caution. Two men had been overtaken and killed here; he didn't propose to be the third.

He halted deliberately and scanned the tortuous descending trail which he had just covered. Then he knew how Daniels and the Swede had been killed. The back trail commanded the gulch so that a pursuer some distance behind in trail distance would still be within fair rifle shot.

It was the danger spot of the homeward trip, he knew, but there was no reason to delay. He moved on into the gulch, keeping a close watch above and to the rear. Almost immediately he saw the movement he had suspected. Someone was in ambush up there on that upper ledge where the trail started down.

He drove Useless into the trees just as a rifle spoke from above, its slug whining from the rocky floor of the trail. Tom let the horse go on into the fringe of scrub pines, remaining himself at the edge of the trail. He reached back with a feeler shot even as the unknown rifleman sent another slug searching for his quarry. Then he saw two riders come down the trail from above, passing out of sight behind the bend of the gulch.

He was in a trap. That rifleman on the ledge could keep him pinned here until those two riders could close in on the lower level. Meanwhile his carbine was hopelessly outranged by the rifle of the man above.

He watched the bend carefully, wondering whether the horsemen would blunder out into view or whether they would dismount and try to flank him across the face of the hill. Either way he determined to make somebody pay before they got him.

A dead silence settled over the gulch and Tom listened intently for the sounds which he knew would precede a flank attack. For long minutes nothing happened, then his alert ear caught a crackle of brush directly down the gulch.

He swung the carbine, lining the sights deliberately on a swaying branch in a clump of laurels. Then he grunted in amazement as the fair hair of Karen Neilson appeared above the thicket.

"The reserves have arrived, General," she called softly. "Where's the enemy?"

His quick annoyance gave way to relief.

"You ought to be spanked for getting into a mess like this," he told her — "but that can wait 'til later. Wiggle over this way and we'll trade guns."

He worked across to meet her and handed her the carbine. "Watch the hillside above and the trail out there. I'm going to surprise that hombre on the ledge."

He checked the Henry's sights and inspected the magazine and chamber before crawling back to his original post. Then he sighted carefully on the bush where his opponent had been. His first shot brought a quick return but swift action came from the second. There was a threshing in the brush up there on the ledge and a man limped out into the open for a moment, only to disappear into the timber.

At the same moment Karen slammed a shot up the ravine. There was just time for Tom to see a horseman wheeling back out of sight, then the flurry of hoof-beats told of a retreat.

"Hit him?" he asked.

"I tried," she said seriously. "It chased him if it didn't do anything else."

"Let's go," he said shortly. "They'll be back soon enough. Where's your horse?"

"Down the gulch. I played Indian when I heard the shooting."

He swung into the saddle and gave her a hand up behind him. "Hold on tight," he grinned. "I like it."

"I wouldn't have guessed it," she retorted. "You seemed more pleased to see the rifle than you did to see me."

"The vanity of woman!" he exclaimed mockingly. "I suppose you think you could throw a slug up there to that ledge? . . . Well, if it will make you feel any happier I'll tell you that you probably saved my hide by arriving when you did."

"You can depend on the reserves," she replied. "How did your search come out?"

"Why do you think they're so anxious to catch me?" he countered. "Balance your gun across the back of the saddle and reach into my right-hand pants pocket. There's the answer."

"Not enough hands to do so many things," she laughed. "I'll take your word. The important thing is that we now have the funds to buy the cattle."

"There are two excellent chances that we won't buy cows with these rocks," he told her, half jokingly. "One possibility is that I'll recover the pelts. I had a bright idea about them last night and if I'm right we'll save the diamonds for the wedding. You might as well have the fun of a big show before you buckle down to being cook for the spread."

"I'll get along," she smiled. "What's the other chance?"

"Maybe we won't get to use them for anything. Unless I miss my guess there will be some pretty tough hombres coming along after them before many minutes. They've been through too much to pass up their chance of a quick fortune now."

CHAPTER
TWENTY-FOUR

They let the horses have their heads going down into White Water Valley. It was no time for dilly-dallying. Hogan would be rallying his men for another attack and there was work to be done in preparing for it.

"Better get some grub ready," Tom suggested as they dismounted before the cabin. "I'm about ready to cave in."

"Always a cook!" she grimaced. "I'm beginning to think you were serious about that part of the deal."

"Sure I was," he said, grabbing the water buckets and starting for the creek. "Better cook plenty. No telling when we'll have time for preparing more food."

It didn't take them long to put the cabin in a state of defense. Karen had left the shutters in place when she rode into the hills so the principal chore was the placing of ammunition and the strengthening of the door. This time there wouldn't be any fooling; it would be a fight to the finish.

The sun was still a good two hours high when a scurry of hoofs sounded from the upper valley. Tom watched from outside, puzzled that a single rider should approach so openly.

"Watch the other sides," he called to Karen. "This might be a ruse."

Then the unknown broke out into the clearing, a small man clinging frantically to a remarkably large horse. It was Dombrek, the surveyor, riding the big bay which had belonged to Daniels.

He tried to raise his hand in a signal of peace but he was having to use both hands to keep himself on the horse. Tom lowered his carbine when the man's helplessness became apparent, waiting to see what this new move meant. Dombrek circled the clearing and gradually pulled the bay down under control. By that time Shelby would have laid odds that he could explain the surveyor's presence. The break had come between Bonsall and Hogan.

He stood watching quietly as Dombrek practically fell from the saddle. There was a smear of blood on the man's left arm but he seemed to use the arm as though it were not seriously injured. Obviously he was more concerned over his back trail. "Better get ready for a fight," he said, his eyes still showing their panic. "They can't be very far behind me."

Tom noted the gun which the bony little man still held in one hand. "You have a tangle with them?"

Dombrek nodded. He seemed surprised to find the gun in his hand. He looked at it curiously for a moment, then thrust it into the holster. "Empty," he said. "I left camp in such a hurry I didn't bring extra ammunition."

Tom took the bay's reins and moved him over to the hitching rail where he would serve to protect Useless.

238

In case lead started flying it would be some consolation to know that the roan had some sort of breastwork on the attacking side.

Then he strode back toward the door of the cabin, motioning for Dombrek to enter. "Let's hear the yarn quick," he said. "I'd like to know what's up before the fun starts."

Dombrek eyed him narrowly. "I guess you know most of it already. This morning I woke up to the sound of shooting. There was nobody in camp but Captain Bonsall and I. We got our horses right away and started up toward where the shooting had been. Pretty soon we found the body of Blackie Steele. It didn't grieve us very much. Then Baldy Wier came pelting down the valley, headed for camp. He said you had found the Neilson woman's bag and that the other men were on your trail. He had been sent back to camp for extra ammunition. Bonsall cussed a blue streak and we started up into the pass."

A rifle bullet crashed through one of the west end shutters, sending the splinters flying. "Here we go," Tom said grimly. "Keep away from the windows; those splinters will do more damage than bullets."

Having thus given good safe advice he proceeded to ignore it. Going to the window which had just been punctured he watched from the loophole for a few moments, then poked the rifle muzzle out and took a careful shot.

"Missed!" he growled. "Go on with your story, Dombrek. What happened when dear brother Bonsall found he had been double-crossed by bigger crooks than himself?"

"He was mad. He had been getting more and more out of humor ever since he failed to find that bag. Then when Hogan began his tricks Bonsall was worried. He was afraid outright robbery and murder would catch up with him."

"I'll bet!" Tom growled. "He's a queer kind of an outlaw. Where's the honest fellow now?"

"He's dead. We came across the men in the pass and Captain Bonsall started to cuss them out proper like he always did. Pew was nursing a wounded leg and it seemed to make him short-tempered. Anyway, he and Bonsall cussed each other and then Pew pulled a gun and killed Bonsall without a bit of warning."

"Breaks my heart," Shelby murmured, studying a suspicious movement in the edge of the woods. He blazed away with a trial shot and asked casually, "How did you make out to get away from them?"

"I had been looking for some kind of a break. When Bonsall started to cuss I started to edge away. Fortunately I was on the best horse in the outfit and when the break came I was able to get away with only a little nick on my arm. That's when I emptied my gun."

Tom took the hint. "I reckon you'll find caps and cartridges there on the table that'll fit it. Load up and take the door. Karen, are you keeping an eye on the corrals?"

"All quiet on this side," she replied steadily. "How many of them do we have to account for now?"

240

"I make it four," Tom grinned. "That's better odds than we had hoped. I reckon there's no use hoping they'll kill off any more of each other."

Dombrek looked around. "Then you knew that Daniels and Svenson were dead?"

"Sure. We saw their bodies. How did it happen?"

"I don't know. The two of them were mighty thick with Pew and Hogan but yesterday morning they were gone from camp when we woke up. Hogan and Pew went after them, cussing at the tops of their lungs. They came back in the afternoon with a yarn that Daniels and the Swede had been killed in a fight over here. They said Daniels had been trying to kidnap Miss Neilson."

Tom fired from his loophole again and let out a whoop of excitement. "Hey! I stirred up somebody that time! Too bad I didn't get down a mite lower."

A slug bored into the north side wall and Tom moved over there, studying the puff of smoke above the bushes before he reached out with an experimental shot. Maybe he was wasting ammunition but there was always the chance of a hit and meanwhile he was keeping them away from the house. It would never do to let Pew get too close with that uncanny rifle of his; he could hit the loopholes at any sort of medium range.

There was an abrupt end to the shooting as dusk began to close down. The defenders fidgeted at their positions, trying to imagine what would happen next and straining their eyes for the sight of a target. It was particularly nerve-racking for Shelby because he had been building up a definite impression that this silence meant something more than a mere delay. Hogan had not yet appeared anywhere around the clearing and Tom was about ready to believe that the others were putting on a show to cover Hogan's move.

He was about to turn from the loophole when Karen uttered a short exclamation. At the same time a whistle shrilled from down the valley. At the signal a horseman came charging out of the bushes and Tom smiled grimly against the stock of his carbine. This was it. They had waited until dusk had come to make shooting more difficult for the defenders. In the split second before he squeezed the trigger Tom was aware of several odd facts. He knew that both Karen and Dombrek were firing, indicating that it was a general assault from all sides at once. That meant a chance of a break through on the one undefended side.

He was also conscious of the identity of the man coming there on the horse. It was the bald man of Bonsall's camp — and he was actually cross-eyed. Tom sighted carefully, waiting only to see the man sprawl from the horse before going across to the single window on the undefended north side.

Karen fired again as he moved, her exclamation of disgust telling of a miss. Tom took a quick glance through the north side loophole and discovered the clearing to be clear of attackers. Hurriedly he moved on toward the door where Dombrek was shooting steadily. Over Dombrek's head he could see a rider galloping in toward the cabin. It was Ike Pew, riding low and firing as he came. A bullet nicked the door frame as Shelby pushed his rifle out through the crack. He flinched as a splinter cut his cheek, then he drew fine and slammed a shot at Pew, sending the man sideways to the ground.

"That's two," he said grimly, levering a fresh shell into the chamber. "What happened to the other two?"

Karen fired again as though in reply. "There's a man out here near the corral," she called. "I hit him when he tried to rush the cabin but I don't think he's seriously hurt."

As if to advertise his own health the unknown blasted another hole in the shutter above her head. "Maybe it's Hogan," Tom said, slipping across to take her place at the loophole.

She moved aside to give him room but it was Dombrek who replied to the remark. "Hogan was on this side with Pew," he said. "They were riding together when they started the attack but Hogan went back and disappeared in the trees."

Tom was watching the corral. "Where did this friend of yours disappear to, cookie?" he asked.

Karen boxed his ears gently. "Stop the cookie business! He's out there where a big pine stands in a cluster of little ones."

Tom stared into the gathering dusk, trying to pick out a flicker of movement in the pines. He was just about to turn away when another slug thudded into the log wall in front of him. He drew a quick bead on the cloud of smoke and fired. There was just time for him to see a stocky figure sliding to the ground. Then the smoke from his own rifle blocked the view.

He turned to grin quietly at Karen. "I reckon we're not doing so bad, cook — er — I mean Karen. That's three of them accounted for and my guess is that Hogan has already left us. He's on his way to recover those pelts. Now that the rest of his game is ruined he'll try to salvage what he can by going back for them."

"Going back?" she repeated.

"Sure. I was just about as dumb on that count as I was about the Indian moving day. There was only one reason why Daniels and Svenson should be killed. They were trying to double-cross the others and get the pelts for themselves. They were headed this way so it was a fair guess that the furs had been cached this side of the pass. I finally woke up to where they must be. Now I've got to get out there before Hogan can get away."

Dombrek's voice interrupted him, a new menacing note in his whining tones. "You ain't goin' anywhere just yet, mister! Before anything else happens you're passing over a neat little bag of diamonds!"

The .44 in his hand wavered between Karen and Tom, its motion a more convincing threat than mere steadiness. Dombrek was nervous; it wouldn't take much to make him shoot.

Tom stared at him in astonishment. The sudden turn was not in itself surprising but the man's words betrayed a knowledge of what he was after. He hadn't talked about a map or gold; he had talked about diamonds!

"You're making a bit of a mistake, ain't you?" Tom remarked, stalling in hopes of some kind of break.

"Don't try to kid me! I've been kicked around long enough on this deal. Last fall I planned to come out here and steal those gems from Neilson. First the

Indians spoiled my plans, then Bonsall got crazy ideas about a gold mine. By that time I knew I was in for something more than just a regular diamond stealing job."

Tom grinned sympathetically. "Tough country for tinhorn crooks," he said. "Did you steal the surveying tools or do you really know something about it?"

The gun was pointing at him now. Dombrek was cagy, realizing that the conversation was intended to cover some sort of break. Still the man couldn't resist the temptation to brag. "These bad hombres out here in the west are tough in their own way but they're dumb. Not one of 'em knew what was in that bag — and none of 'em suspected that I'd kill them the moment they found it. I was just a greenhorn to be pitied — but now I hold all the aces. Just hand the stones over and I might let you go in time to save your furs from that Hogan rat."

Out of the corner of his eye Tom could see that Karen was letting her hand work toward a frying pan which hung on a nail. If Dombrek caught her at that he would shoot instantly. Tom spoke quickly, trying to keep the man's attention. "Looks like you win," he conceded. "I reckon we'd better make terms so I can get on Hogan's trail. Better to have the furs than to have neither."

Dombrek nodded eagerly. "That's being smart. Just hand over the stones and . . ." It wasn't hard to judge that no one would leave this cabin to tell the story. The only reason Dombrek hadn't killed them both without warning was that he didn't know where the diamonds had been placed.

Still Tom pretended. "Want me to get 'em out of my pocket or are you afraid I've got a hideout gun?" He tapped the bulge on his right thigh.

Dombrek's eyes followed the move and in that split second of diversion Karen made her play. The frying pan caught Dombrek full in the face and Tom went in with a flying dive as the surveyor's gun wavered. The weapon boomed in Shelby's ear but the shot did no damage. In a twinkling the little man was tied up and Karen was replacing her frying pan on the wall as though nothing remarkable had happened. Only when she turned to face Shelby in the gloom did she speak. "If you make any humorous remarks about cooks I'll use it on *you*!" she warned.

His arm circled her shoulders happily. "I don't know who's in worse shape," he said, "Jeff or me. He's got a woman who busts men over the head with chairs. I've got one who throws frying pans. What a life!"

She laughed a little nervously but with more than a trace of proud satisfaction. He held her closely for a moment, then released her and spoke briskly again. "Time to ride," he said. "This looks like the big night for a clean-up. If I can just catch Hogan we'll be in the clear on all counts."

"Let's go," she said simply. "I've been in on this much; I don't propose to miss the final act."

246

CHAPTER
TWENTY-FIVE

He stood silent in the darkness for a couple of minutes, trying to decide where the danger now lay. Then he said shortly, "We'll argue that point later. Right now I'd better look to those jaspers outside. Can't have wounded men lying around even if they are coyotes like these. Watch Dombrek carefully; if he so much as wiggles crown him with that frying pan again."

Alone outside he had a chance to think things over. He didn't want Karen to ride with him when he went to face Hogan, yet he couldn't leave her here alone. Dombrek might get free, Hogan might double back or one of those wounded men might recover enough to take her by surprise. He had to avoid any such danger as that even if the extra caution did result in Hogan getting away with the pelts.

He swung around the corner of the cabin to the west, quickly coming upon the body of the bald man. The fellow was dead and Tom didn't pause except to pick up the fallen rifle and six-gun. A circuit of the corral brought him to the edge of the timber where the red-whiskered bandit lay half hidden by the pines. He too was stone dead and Tom felt a sense of relief. There

The men followed silently, pausing only for a question when they passed the body of Pew. Shelby grinned thinly. "Think nothing of it. There's dead men all around."

"Good or bad?" Coulter asked.

Karen took it upon herself to answer that one from the doorway. "Good ones" — she said distinctly — "good ones to be dead. Unless Dombrek lied to us he's the only survivor of Bonsall's worthy company."

Andrews grunted in surprise at sight of the bound man. "Too bad you didn't make it unanimous," he declared. "How come ropes instead of lead?"

Karen was smiling in fine spirits at sight of the friendly faces around her. These were the men who had done so much for her before. Now they were back again when help was needed. "We saved him for you," she said cryptically. "You might be able to turn him into cash."

Shelby smothered an exclamation of surprise. "Maybe you're right!" he said. "If he's a smart enough jewel thief to plan a job like this and carry it out the way he did — and come so close to getting away with it — there's a good chance that he has a price on his head somewhere."

Karen smiled with pleasure. "So he's yours," she said to the troopers. "Take good care of him and find the right police department."

It took more explanation than that for Andrews and his men to understand the chain of events which had brought a gem thief into the hills posing as a faint-hearted tenderfoot. It wasn't until some time later

250

that Coulter found a chance to break in with his story, the story which had brought these men back to White Water Valley.

"Look, Shelby," he exploded impatiently at the first break in the talk. "I've got a hunch about those pelts. It was just a hunch at first but when we found Hogan down the valley I was dead sure I was right. He knew his secret was out, too, 'cause he opened fire without askin' any questions."

"Good figuring, Jim," Shelby approved quietly. "You got it without a hint, I see. I didn't tumble until Daniels and Svenson were killed."

Coulter looked disappointed. "Then you figured it out?"

Tom nodded but Karen broke in impatiently. "Will you please stop being so mysterious? You talked like that once before and I still don't know what happened to the furs."

"Oldest stunt in the hills," he grinned. "The thieves buried them when they camped for the night. Probably piled the dirt on a blanket as they dug it up, carrying it to the creek so it wouldn't show. Then they built their fire over the cache itself and picketed the horses so their hoof marks would cover the sign they had made in taking the soil to the creek. Maybe we were tired, maybe they did a good job but anyway we somehow missed the cache."

She nodded her comprehension. "Then Daniels and his partner were killed by the others when they tried to sneak away and steal the furs for themselves?"

"Right enough, I reckon. As it stands we get our own back and recover Dutchy's for him as well."

He grinned a little ruefully. "I hope I'm not counting my pelts before they're recovered. I felt pretty sure of my theory when Hogan sneaked away from the other fellows this evening."

"You got it," Coulter told him. "Hogan was digging in the campfire spot when we run across him."

"Fair enough. Tomorrow I'll ask you boys to help me and we'll pack 'em in to the fort."

Andrews grinned meaningly. "We'll take 'em. Now that you've got everything under control I reckon you'd rather have us go 'way and leave you alone."

Shelby was elaborately casual. "I guess we'll go along. The squarehead here has been proposing to me between fights so I reckon I'll have to marry her. Cooks are hard to get."

For all his pretense of carelessness he was watching for just the move she made. As she reached out for the frying pan he leaped to pin both of her arms to her sides. His mouth and nose were being tickled by hair which shone golden in the lamplight but he managed a quick grin at the troopers. "How would you boys like to go bury some two-legged coyotes?" he asked solemnly. "I've got to make peace here or we won't get any grub."

COUNTY LIBRARY SERVICE
ROSCOMMON

Roscommon County Library Service

WITHDRAWN
FROM STOCK